13

'Need me to prove that you still want me?'

His mouth came down on hers with seductive intent, and immediately she sank against him—because no one kissed like Alessandro, and resisting him was impossible. His kiss was hungry and primitive, and she clutched at him, pressing against him, her need so intense that she forgot everything except her desire for him.

Then he released her and stepped back, his expression cold. 'The children need both their parents. We're a family, Christy, and that isn't going to change. And don't pretend you don't want me.'

Oh, she wanted him. How could she pretend otherwise when her nipples were pressing hard against the soft material of her scrub suit and her mouth was still swollen from the ravages of his kiss?

She wanted him. But how did she explain that she needed more than the physical when his solution to every problem was sex?

And the fact that he'd made it clear that his thoughts were only for the children caused her intense pain. He would stay married to her for the sake of the children.

Could she do the same? Could she stay with him, knowing that he didn't love her any more?

Dear Reader

Two years ago I wrote a mountain rescue trilogy based in the Lake District, and I enjoyed the experience so much I couldn't resist the temptation to return to the same place.

In the first book, my heroine, Christy, agrees to spend Christmas with her estranged husband, Alessandro, for the sake of the children—even though their marriage is in crisis. Their passionate relationship has become fractured through lack of communication, and it seems that nothing can save it. But they are given a little outside help from their two children and their friend Jake. This book is very special to me, because my own children provided much of the inspiration and dialogue.

Having developed a secondary character as delicious as Jake, there was no way I could abandon him! So the second book is his story. Faced with the prospect of spending yet another Christmas alone, Jake goes for a walk in the mountains, where he encounters Miranda. But, as so often happens in life, things aren't as they seem. Will Jake be able to accept the person she really is? And will Miranda be able to learn to trust him?

This duo contains a cast of characters who will be familiar to many of my readers, including Sean Nicholson, my very first hero, who is still very alive in my head. Fortunately he is ageing well, and is still as attractive as ever.

Love

Sarah xx

THE CHRISTMAS MARRIAGE RESCUE

BY
SARAH MORGAN

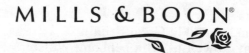

MILLS & BOON®

First published in Great Britain 2006
Large Print edition 2007
Harlequin Mills & Boon Limited,
Eton House, 18-24 Paradise Road,
Richmond, Surrey TW9 1SR

© Sarah Morgan 2006

ISBN-13: 978 0 263 19347 3
ISBN-10:   0 263 19347 0

Set in Times Roman 16½ on 20 pt.
17-0507-51204

Printed and bound in Great Britain
by Antony Rowe Ltd, Chippenham, Wiltshire

Sarah Morgan trained as a nurse, and has since worked in a variety of health-related jobs. Married to a gorgeous businessman, who still makes her knees knock, she spends most of her time trying to keep up with their two little boys, but manages to sneak off occasionally to indulge her passion for writing romance. Sarah loves outdoor life, and is an enthusiastic skier and walker. Whatever she is doing, her head is always full of new characters, and she is addicted to happy endings.

Recent titles by the same author:

GIFT OF A FAMILY
THE SICILIAN DOCTOR'S PROPOSAL
MILLION-DOLLAR LOVE-CHILD*
HIGH-ALTITUDE DOCTOR

*Mills & Boon® Modern Romance™

For my parents, with love.

And thanks to my children
for providing endless authentic dialogue
and for proving that any bed can be broken
if you bounce hard enough.

PROLOGUE

'Mum, where are we spending Christmas?'

Christy glanced up from the letter she was reading. 'I don't know. Here, I suppose, with Uncle Pete and your cousins. Why do you ask? Christmas is ages away.' And she was trying not to think about it. Christmas was a time for families and hers appeared to be disintegrating.

And it was all her fault. She'd done a *really* stupid thing and now they were all paying the price.

'Christmas is a month away. Not ages.' Katy leaned across the table and snatched the cereal packet from her little brother. 'And I don't want to stay here. I love Uncle Pete, but I hate London. I want to spend Christmas with Dad in the Lake District. I want to go home.'

Christy felt her insides knot with anguish. They wanted to spend Christmas with their father?

She just couldn't begin to imagine spending Christmas without the children. 'All right.' Her voice was husky and she cleared her throat. 'Of course, that's fine, if you're sure that's what you want.' *Oh, dear God, how would she survive?* What would Christmas morning be without the children? 'I'll write to your father and tell him that you're both coming up to stay. You might need to spend some time at Grandma's because Daddy will be working at the hospital, of course, and it's always a busy time for the mountain rescue team and—'

'Not just us.' Katy reached for the sugar. 'I didn't mean that we go without you. That would be hideous. I meant that we all go.'

'What do you mean, all? And that's enough sugar, Katy. You'll rot your teeth.'

'They go into *holes*,' Ben breathed, with the gruesome delight of a seven-year-old. He picked up the milk jug and tried to pour milk into his cup but succeeded in slopping most of it over the table. 'I learned about it in school last week. You eat sugar, you get *holes*. Then the dentist has to drill a bigger hole and fill it with cement.'

'You are so lame! What do you know about anything, anyway?' Katy threw her brother a disdainful look and doubled the amount of sugar she was putting on her cereal. 'Stupid, idiot baby.'

'I'm not a baby! I'm seven!' Ben shot out of his chair and made a grab at his sister, who immediately put her hands round his throat.

'*Why* did I have to be lumbered with a brother?'

'Stop it, you two! Not his throat, Katy,' Christy admonished, her head starting to thump as she reached for a cloth and mopped up the milk on the table. 'You know that you don't put anything round each other's throats. You might strangle him.'

'That was the general idea,' Katy muttered, glaring at Ben before picking up her spoon and digging into her cereal. 'Anyway, as I was saying. I don't want Ben and I to go home for Christmas, I want all three of us to go.'

The throb in Christy's head grew worse and she rose to her feet in search of paracetamol. 'This is home now, sweetheart.' Thanks to her stupidity. 'London is home now.'

As if to remind herself of that depressing fact, she stared out of the window of their tiny flat, through the sheeting rain and down into the road below. There was a steady hiss as the traffic crawled along the wet, cheerless street. Brick buildings, old, tired and in need of repainting, rose up high, blocking out what there was of the restrained winter light. People shouted abuse and leaned on their horns and all the time the rain fell steadily, dampening streets and spirits with equal effectiveness. On the pavement people jostled and dodged, ears glued to mobile phones, walking and talking, eyes straight ahead, no contact with each other.

And then, just for a moment, the reality disappeared and Christy had a vision of the Lake District. Her real home. The sharp edges of the fells rising up against a perfectly blue sky on a crisp winter morning. The clank of metal and the sound of laughter as the mountain rescue team prepared for another callout. Friendship.

Oh, dear God, she didn't want to be here. *This wasn't how it was supposed to have turned out.*

As if picking up her mood, Ben's face crumpled as he flopped back into his chair. 'It isn't home. It'll never be home, it's horrid and I hate it. I hate London, I hate school and most of all I hate you.' And with that he scraped his chair away from the table and belted out of the door, sobbing noisily, leaving his cereal untouched.

Feeling sick with misery, Christy watched him go, suppressing a desperate urge to follow and give him a cuddle but knowing from experience that it was best to let him calm down in his own time. She sat back down at the table and tried to revive her flagging spirits. It was seven-thirty in the morning, she had to get two children to a school that they hated and she had to go on to a job that she hated, too. What on earth was she doing?

She topped up her coffee-cup and tried to retrieve the situation. 'London at Christmas will be pretty cool.'

Katy shot her a pitying look. 'Mum, *don't* try and communicate on my level. It's tragic when grown-ups do that. *I* can say cool, but it sounds ridiculous coming from anyone over the age of sixteen. Use grown-up words like "interesting" or "exciting". Leave "cool" and "wicked" to those of us who appreciate the true meaning.' With all the vast superiority of her eleven years, she pushed her bowl to one side and reached for a piece of toast. 'And, anyway, it won't be cool. The shopping's good, but you can only do so much of that.'

Christy wondered whether she ought to point out that so far her daughter hadn't shown any signs of tiring of that particular occupation but decided that the atmosphere around the breakfast table was already taut enough. 'I can't go back to the Lake District this Christmas,' she said finally, and Katy lifted the toast to her lips.

'Why not? Because you and Dad have had a row?' She shrugged. 'What's new?'

Christy bit her lip and reflected on the challenges of having a daughter who was growing up and saw too much. She picked up her coffee-cup, determined to be mature about the whole thing. 'Katy, we didn't—'

'Yes, you did, but it's hardly surprising, is it? He's Spanish and you're half-Irish with red hair. Uncle Pete says that makes for about as explosive combination as it's possible to get. I suppose things might have been different if you'd been born a blonde.' Katy chewed thoughtfully.

'Amazing, really, that the two of you managed to get it together for long enough to produce us.'

Christy choked on her coffee and made a mental note to have a sharp talk with her brother. 'Katy, that's enough.'

'I'm just pointing out that the fact that you two can't be in a room without trying to kill each other is no reason to keep us down here in London. We hate it, Mum. It's great seeing Uncle Pete but a short visit is plenty. You hate it, too, I know you do.'

Was it that obvious? 'I have a job here.' In the practice where her brother worked as a GP. And it was fine, she told herself firmly. Fine. Perfectly adequate. She was lucky to have it.

'You're a nurse, Mum. You can get a job anywhere.'

Oh, to be a child again, when everything seemed so simple and straightforward. 'Katy—'

'Just for Christmas. Please? Don't you miss Dad?'

The knot was back in her stomach. Christy closed her eyes and saw dark, handsome features. An arrogant, possessive smile and a mouth that could bring her close to madness. *Oh, yes.* Oh, yes, she missed him dreadfully. And, at this distance, some of her anger had faded. But the hurt was still there. All right, so she'd been stupid but she wouldn't have done it if he hadn't been so—so *aggravating.* 'I can't discuss my relationship with your father with you.'

'I'm eleven,' Katy reminded her. 'I know about relationships. And I know that the two of you are stubborn.'

He hadn't contacted her. Pride mingled with pain and Christy pressed her lips together to stop a sob escaping. He was *supposed* to have followed her. Dragged her back. He was supposed to have fought for what they had. But he hadn't even been in touch except when they made arrangements about the children. *He didn't care that she'd gone.* The knowledge sat like a heavy weight in her heart and stomach. Suddenly she felt a ridiculous urge to confide in her child but she knew that she couldn't do that, no matter how grown-up Katy seemed. 'I can't spend Christmas with your father.'

She'd started this but she didn't know how to

finish it. He was supposed to have finished it. He was supposed to have come after her. That was why she'd left. To try and make him listen. 'A wake-up call', a marriage counsellor would probably call it.

'If I have a row with one of my friends you always say, "Sit down, Katy, and discuss it like a grown-up."' Katy rolled her eyes, her imitation next to perfect. 'And what do you do? You move to opposite ends of the country. Hardly a good example to set, is it?'

Christy stiffened and decided that some discipline was called for. 'I'm not sure I like your tone.'

'And I'm not sure I like being the product of a broken home.' Katy finished her toast and took a sip from her glass of milk. 'Goodness knows what it will do to me. You read about it every day in the papers. There's a strong chance I'm going to go off the rails. Theft. Pregnancy—'

Christy banged her cup down onto the table. 'What do you know about pregnancy?'

Katy shot her a pitying look. 'Oh, get a life, Mum. I know plenty.'

'You do?' She just wasn't ready to handle this

stage of child development on her own, Christy thought weakly. She needed Alessandro. She needed—

Oh, help…

'And don't write to him. Ring him up.' Katy glanced at the clock and stood up, ponytail swinging. 'We'd better go or we'll be late. The traffic never moves in this awful place. I've never spent so many hours standing still in my whole life and I don't think I can stand it any more. I'll ring him if you're too cowardly.'

'I'm not cowardly.' Or maybe she was. He hadn't rung her. Gorgeous, sexy Alessandro, who was always wrapped up in his job or his role on the mountain rescue team, always the object of a million women's fantasies. Once she'd been wrapped up in the same things but then the children had come and somehow she'd been left behind…

And he didn't notice her any more. He didn't have time for their relationship. *For her.*

'Ben's upstairs, crying. I'm here eating far too much sugar and you're ingesting a lethal dose of caffeine,' Katy said dramatically as she walked to the door, her performance worthy of the

London stage. 'We're a family in crisis. We need our father or *goodness knows* what might happen to us.'

Christy didn't know whether to laugh or cry. 'You haven't finished your milk,' she said wearily. 'All right, I'll talk to him. See what he says.'

It would be just for the festive season, she told herself. The children shouldn't suffer because of her stupidity and Alessandro's arrogant, stubborn nature.

'Really?'

'Really.'

'Yay!' Katy punched the air, her ponytail swinging. 'We're going back to the Lake District for Christmas. Snow. Rain. Howling winds. I'll see my old friends. My phone bill will plummet. Thanks Mum, you're the best.'

As she danced out of the room, no doubt *en route* to pass the joyful news on to her brother, Christy felt her stomach sink down to her ankles. Now all she had to do was summon the courage to phone Alessandro and tell him that they were planning to return home for Christmas.

How on earth was she going to do that?

CHAPTER ONE

'EMERGENCY on its way in, Mr Garcia.' The pretty nurse stuck her head round the office door. 'You're needed in Resus.'

Alessandro dropped the report on staffing that he was reading and wondered how many times a day he heard that statement. He was always needed in Resus. Sometimes he felt as though he lived in Resus. Particularly at the moment when almost forty per cent of the staff were off with flu.

He strode out of his office, nodded to one of the A and E sisters who hurried past him, looking harassed, and shouldered his way through the double doors into Resus.

Chaos reigned.

'She's bleeding from somewhere, we need to find out where.' Billy, one of the casualty officers, was trying to direct operations and he looked up with a sigh of relief as Alessandro appeared by the side of the trolley. 'Oh, Mr Garcia. Thank goodness. Dr Nicholson is already tied up with that climbing accident and—'

'What's the story?' Alessandro cut him off and Billy sucked in a breath.

'Her husband brought her in by car. She was complaining of abdominal pain all night and he was driving quickly in an attempt to get her here and took the car into the ditch.' Clearly out of his comfort zone, he dragged a hand through his hair, leaving it more untidy than ever. 'She's had a bang on her head and her obs suggests that she's bleeding but we don't know where from.'

Alessandro took the gloves that a nurse was holding out to him and made a mental note to speak to Billy about the quality of his handover skills at some point in the near future.

'Does "she" have a name?' he enquired softly and Billy coloured.

'Megan. Megan Yates.'

Alessandro swiftly dragged on the gloves and turned to the woman who was lying on the trolley, noted her pale, blood-streaked cheeks and the fear in her eyes. 'Megan, this must be very frightening for you, but you're in hospital now and we're going to make you comfortable as quickly as we can.' He lifted his gaze to Billy. 'Bleep the on-call gynae team,' he instructed calmly, donning the rest of the necessary protective clothing and glancing at the monitor. 'We need to keep an eye on her pulse and blood pressure.'

Her pulse was up, her blood pressure was dropping and she was showing all the signs of haemorrhage. But, unlike his less experienced colleague, he had no intention of sharing his concerns with an already worried patient.

Billy followed his gaze. 'The gynae team?' His tone was level but his expression was confused. 'I thought after an RTA and trauma, she'd need—'

'And she's of childbearing age, and before her husband landed the car in the ditch she was suffering from abdominal pain,' Alessandro reminded him, 'so that is not to be forgotten. I want two lines in her straight away, wide-bore cannulae.'

Responding immediately to his decisive tone, Nicky, one of the A and E sisters, pushed a trolley across Resus and Billy put a tourniquet on the woman's arm and ripped open the first cannula. 'You think she might have a ruptured ectopic?'

'I don't know yet, but let's just say I have a low threshold of suspicion so I'm treating it as that until I have reason to think otherwise.' Alessandro continued to deliver a steady stream of instructions while the staff around him bobbed and moved in perfect unison. They were so used to working together that they often anticipated each other's needs. He turned back to his patient. 'Megan, is there any chance that you could be pregnant?'

'No—well, I mean…' The woman closed her eyes briefly. 'It's so unlikely it's virtually impossible.'

'In this department we deal with the unlikely and the impossible on a fairly regular basis,' Alessandro replied with a wry smile. 'When was your last period?'

'Months ago,' she whispered. 'I have endometriosis.'

He heard the catch in her voice and put a hand on her shoulder. 'That must be hard for you,' he said gently. 'But right now we need to find out what injuries you suffered in the accident and try and get to the bottom of your abdominal pain. We need to undress you so that we can do a proper examination, head to toe, and find out exactly what is going on. Nicky?'

Nicky was already removing clothes, fingers and scissors moving swiftly as Alessandro started his examination.

'Where's her husband?' He was checking the body methodically, on the alert for anything life-threatening. 'Was he injured?'

'He's fine,' Billy muttered as he successfully put the second line in and taped it in place. 'Waiting in the relatives' room. Nicky put him there.'

'She has a nasty laceration of her shoulder.' Nicky reached for a sterile pad while Alessandro examined it swiftly.

'That's going to need stitching but it can wait,' he murmured, his gaze sliding to the monitor again. 'Her pressure is still dropping. I want to know why. And I want to know now. Did someone bleep the gynae team?'

'On their way,' a staff nurse reported and Alessandro's eyes narrowed.

He didn't like the look of his patient.

'Oh…' Nicky finished cutting off the woman's clothes and her face reflected shock before she quickly masked it. 'We have some blood loss here, Alessandro.'

One glance was all it took for him to measure the degree of the understatement. 'Fast-bleep Jake Blackwell,' he ordered in a calm voice. 'Cross-match six units of blood and get her rhesus status. We may need to give her anti-D. And someone get a blanket on her before she gets hypothermia.'

Jake Blackwell, the consultant obstetrician, strode into the room minutes later. 'You need my advice, Garcia? Struggling?' His eyes mocked but Alessandro was too worried about his patient to take the bait.

'I need you to do some work for a change,' he drawled, but although his tone was casual and relaxed, his eyes were sharp and alert and his handover to his colleague was so succinct that Billy threw him a look of admiration.

Jake listened, examined the woman swiftly and then nodded, all traces of humour gone. 'Megan, it looks as though you might have an ectopic pregnancy—that means that the egg has implanted somewhere other than your uterus and, in your case, it seems that it may have done some damage that we need to put right with an operation.' He lifted his eyes to Alessandro. 'She's going to need surgery. We'll take her straight to Theatre. Damn. I'm supposed to be somewhere else. I need to make a couple of calls—speak to the anaesthetist, juggle my list.'

Alessandro leaned across and increased the flow of both the oxygen and the IV himself. 'Just so long as you juggle it quickly. We'll transfer her to Theatre while you do what you need to do. Her husband is in our relatives' room if you want to tackle the issue of consent.'

'Great.' Jake walked to the phone and punched in a number while Alessandro monitored his patient.

'Phone down and get that blood sent up to Theatre as soon as it's available,' he ordered, and Nicky hurried to the nearest phone to do as he'd instructed.

Minutes later the woman was on her way to

Theatre and Jake disappeared to talk to her husband.

He reappeared in the department hours later, after Alessandro had dealt with what felt like a million road accidents, intermingled with a significant number of people with flu.

'Why don't people stay in bed when they have flu?' he grumbled as Jake appeared in the doorway of his office. 'For a start, if they can get out of bed then it isn't flu and it certainly isn't an accident or an emergency. Why come to a hospital and spread it around?'

'Because they're generous?' Jake strolled into the office and dropped onto the nearest chair without even bothering to move the pile of files that were covering it. 'Hell, I'm knackered. I've spent the whole day in Theatre saving lives. One drama after another. You don't know you're born, working down here.'

Alessandro thought of the two major RTAs, the heart attack and the sickle-cell crisis he'd dealt with since lunchtime. And the only way he'd known it had been lunchtime had been because he'd looked at the clock on the wall. He hadn't eaten for hours. 'That's right. I spend my life sitting on my backside.'

'Backside?' Jake grinned. 'That doesn't sound like a particularly Spanish word, *amigo*.'

Feeling tired and bad-tempered, Alessandro scowled at him. 'Haven't you got anything better to do with your time than sit in my office, moaning?'

'Actually, I came down to see if you fancy grabbing a couple of beers after work. I have a feeling that our problems are nothing that alcohol can't fix.'

Alessandro pulled a face. 'Not tonight.'

Jake yawned. 'You working late?'

'I'm cleaning up the house.' Alessandro felt the tension rise inside him. 'Christy and the kids are arriving tomorrow for Christmas. I need to throw out four months' worth of take-away cartons and fill the fridge with broccoli or she'll hit the roof. You know Christy and her obsession with nutrition.'

Jake stared, his blue eyes suddenly keen and interested. 'You guys are back together?'

'No. We're not back together.' Alessandro all

but snapped the words out, his anger suddenly so close to the surface that his fingers tightened on the pencil he was holding and broke it in two. 'We're spending Christmas in the same house for the sake of the kids.'

'I see.' Jake's eyes rested on the broken pencil, his expression thoughtful. 'Well, that promises to be a peaceful Christmas, then. Better warn Santa to wear his flak jacket when he flies over your barn. Wouldn't want him to be caught in flying shrapnel as you two tear bits off each other.'

Alessandro thought about all the occasions he'd seen Christy in the last six weeks. Brief occasions when they'd handed over the children. They'd barely spoken, let alone rowed. 'It isn't like that any more.' Christmas promised to be as icy cold as the weather and Alessandro was suddenly struck by inspiration. 'Why don't you join us? You're their godfather.'

Jake nodded. 'I might do that if I can drag myself away from the irresistible lure of this place. You know how I am with cold hospital turkey and lumpy gravy. I've been trying to break myself of the addiction for years.' He stretched his legs out in front of him. 'You know, about this thing that's going on with you and Christy—'

'There's nothing going on. We're separated and that's all there is to it. And I don't want to talk about it.' Alessandro's gaze was shuttered and Jake sighed.

'I just hate to see the two of you like this. You're my best friends and if anyone was ever meant to be together, it's you two. You should hang onto what you've got. It's hard enough finding anyone you get on vaguely well with in this world. Christy was crazy about you, right from day one. And you were crazy about her. I remember the day you guys met—'

'I said, I don't want to talk about it,' Alessandro said coldly, his dark eyes stormy and threatening as he rose to his feet and paced over to the window, angry with Jake for stirring up memories that he'd spent ages trying to bury. *How could he ever forget the day he'd first met Christy?*

He stared out of the window. Outside, snow lay thick on the ground, disguising the usually familiar landscape. In the distance the fells rose.

He studied their familiar jagged lines and then turned, his volatile Mediterranean temper bubbling to the surface. 'She left me.'

'I know.' Jake's voice was soft. 'I wonder why she felt she had to do that?'

Alessandro's jaw tensed. 'If you're implying that any of this is my fault, you're wrong.'

'Christy adores you. She's crazy about you and always has been. If she left you, she must have been desperate,' Jake said quietly. 'She must have felt there was no other way to get through to you.'

'That's ridiculous. She could have talked to me.'

Jake's expression was inscrutable. 'Could she? Did you make yourself available?'

Alessandro sucked in a frustrated breath. 'How could we talk when she left me?' He sounded impossibly Spanish and Jake gave a wry smile.

'So is that what this is all about?' His eyes narrowed. 'Pride? She was the one to walk away from you so you're not going to go after her? Why did she leave you, Al?' Jake's voice was calm as he rose to his feet. 'Try asking yourself that question while you're binning take-away cartons.'

And with that parting shot he left the room and closed the door quietly behind him.

Christy had changed her clothes a dozen times and in the end settled on a pencil skirt, a pair of heels and a blue jumper in the softest cashmere, which she'd bought in a small shop on the King's Road to cheer herself up. It hadn't worked, but she knew she looked good in it. And she wanted to remind Alessandro what he was missing. Not that she wanted them to get back together again, she told herself hastily, because she didn't. Oh, no. She wasn't that stupid.

Obviously he wasn't interested in her any more. Their marriage had worn itself out. He was an arrogant, selfish, macho workaholic who suited himself in life and clearly he didn't love her any more. If he'd loved her, he *never* would have let her leave.

As they drove deeper into Cumbria she saw the fells rise under a crown of snow and felt the tension leave her. The winter winds had dragged the last of the leaves from the trees and the sky was grey and menacing but it was wild and familiar. *It was home.*

Why, she wondered, had she thought that she could be happy in London? She'd never been a city girl. For her, life had always been about being outdoors. Being active and close to nature. When Christmas was over, she'd move back up here and find a job in the Lake District. There must be some other department she could work in that didn't have links with Alessandro. She didn't have to throw away everything she loved just because their relationship was on the rocks.

She needed to build a new life.

A life that didn't include Alessandro.

'Mum?' Ben's little voice whined from the back of the car, disturbing her thoughts. 'Are we there yet?'

'Nearly. Don't you recognise those trees?' Christy changed down a gear and took the sharp turning that led down the lane to the barn.

They'd discovered it during the second year of their marriage. Katy had been a baby and they'd both fallen in love with the potential of the old, tumble-down building bordered by fields and a fast-flowing river. They'd spent the next few years living on a building site while they'd lovingly turned it into their dream home.

And there it was, smoke rising from the chimney like a welcome beacon.

Christy swallowed and slowed the car. Except it wasn't a welcome, was it? Alessandro didn't want her any more. He'd made that perfectly clear. For him, their marriage was over. And the fact that they were about to spend three weeks together was everything to do with the children and nothing to do with them.

It was going to be something akin to torture.

She was going to be dignified, she reminded herself as she pulled the car up outside the front of the barn and switched off the engine. They were both civilised human beings. They could spend time together for the sake of their children.

She wasn't going to lose her temper. She wasn't going to show him how upset she was. She wasn't going to reveal that she wished she'd never left. She wasn't going to cry and most of all she wasn't going to let him know that she thought about him day and night.

But then the front door was pulled open and all her resolutions flew out of her head.

Alessandro stood there, his powerful, athletic body almost filling the doorway. He looked dark and dangerous and Christy caught her breath, just as she had on that very first day they'd met. One glance at those brooding dark eyes was enough to make her forget her own name. Wasn't time supposed to put a dent in sexual attraction? she thought helplessly. Wasn't she supposed to have become bored and indifferent over time? Well, it certainly hadn't happened in her case. But that was probably because Alessandro was no ordinary guy, she thought miserably as she switched off the engine and tried to slow the rhythmic thump of her heart. He was strong, un-ashamedly masculine, hotly sexual and almost indecently handsome. The combination was a killer and no woman would ever pass him by without giving a second and third look.

He stood now in his usual arrogant, self-confident pose, legs planted slightly apart, his hair gleaming glossy black in the fading winter sunlight, his shoulders broad and muscular under the thick, ribbed jumper. He wore scuffed walking boots and ancient jeans and she thought, with a lurch of her heart and a sick feeling in the pit of her stomach, that he'd never looked more attractive. And she had absolutely no doubt that other women felt the same way.

He was a red-blooded male with a high sex drive and they hadn't shared a bed for almost two months.

Had he taken a lover?

The thought flew into her head from nowhere and she pushed it away again, too sick at the thought to even dwell on the possibility.

'Dad!' Katy and Ben were out of the car before Christy had a chance to get herself together and suddenly she realised that they were doing what she wanted to do. She wanted to run and hug him. She wanted him to tell her that this was all a ridiculous misunderstanding and hear him tell her that everything was going to be all right.

And then she wanted him to take her to bed and fix everything.

But he didn't even glance towards the car. He just hugged the children and fussed over them, which meant that it was up to her to make the first move.

Thank goodness for the children, she thought miserably as she opened her car door. Because of them, they wouldn't have to spend time as a couple and clearly Alessandro didn't consider them to be a couple any more.

She strolled over to him, glad of the cashmere jumper. It was cold. Significantly colder than London.

He was still hugging the children but their eyes met over the top of two dark little heads.

'Christianne.' His voice was cool, his handsome face blank of expression, and suddenly she wanted to leap at him and claw him just to get a reaction.

How could he seem so indifferent?

How could he call her Christianne in that smooth, formal tone when he only ever called her Christy?

After everything they'd shared—*a fierce, perfect passion*—how could he be so cold towards her?

'Alessandro.' Rat. Snake, she thought to herself. How could you do this to me? *To us?*

'Good journey?' He had a trace of a Spanish accent that he'd never lost despite the fact he'd lived in England for the past twelve years. She'd always loved his accent but suddenly it just seemed like a reminder of the differences between them.

'Fine, thanks. Traffic was pretty heavy coming out of London, but I suppose that's to be expected at this time of year. First day of the Christmas holidays.' She almost winced as she heard herself talking. She sounded so formal. As if they were strangers rather than two people who had shared everything there had been to share for the last twelve years. Any moment now, they'd be shaking hands.

Fortunately Katy grabbed Ben and started to dance a jig. 'No more school,' she sang in a delighted voice. 'No more vile, horrid school with demented, stinky, bullying teachers.'

But Alessandro wasn't looking at the children. He was looking at her, with those hot, dark eyes that were a symbol of his Mediterranean heritage.

She saw his gaze slide down her body and rest on the high-heeled shoes; the shoes that had seemed so pretty in London and now felt utterly ridiculous with snow on the ground and the cold bite of winter in the air. In London, it hadn't felt like winter. It had just felt wet and miserable. The shoes had cheered her up. Given her confidence. *Reminded her that she was a woman.*

Noting his disdainful glance, her confidence evaporated and she knew instinctively that he was thinking about all the people he'd had to rescue from the mountains because they'd been wearing ridiculous footwear. Suddenly she wanted to defend herself. To tell him that she wasn't walking anywhere but that the shoes made her legs look good and she'd wanted him to notice.

Suddenly nervous and not understanding why, she waved a hand at the fells. 'When did it snow?'

'A week ago.' His wry tone said it all and she looked back at him, noting the dark shadows under his eyes with a flash of surprise.

She knew that Alessandro had endless stamina. Why would he look tired?

'I suppose you've been really busy, then.' She almost laughed as she listened to herself. What a stupid thing to say. When was Alessandro ever not busy? Work was his life. As she'd discovered to her cost.

'The weather isn't helping.' He strode over to her car and retrieved the cases from the boot. 'I'm afraid I have to go back to the hospital after you've settled in.'

Katy groaned an instant protest. 'Daddy, no!'

'Sorry, *niña*.' Alessandro stooped and dropped a kiss on his daughter's head. 'There are lots of staff off sick, but I'm sure they'll be better soon. I'll have more time next week and we'll go climbing, that's a promise.'

Christy frowned as she followed him into the barn. 'You're not taking her climbing in this weather, Alessandro.'

'You used to climb in this weather.' His sardonic gaze made her heart tumble.

They'd argued about it so many times. When they'd first met, she'd been young and reckless. He'd been fiercely protective. Possessive. Hadn't wanted her out there in the mountains where danger might exist. And she'd teased him and gone anyway, loving the fact that he cared enough to want to stop her from doing anything remotely dangerous. Provoking him. *Pushing him to the edges of patience.*

'Well, I don't climb now.' Her life was so safe and boring that it was enough to make her scream. She frowned at the thought. It was funny, she mused, how your lifestyle could change so gradually that you didn't even notice it happening. One day you were hanging from a cliff by your fingernails and the next you were wading through a pile of ironing, listening to the radio.

How had it happened?

There'd been a time when she would have tugged on her walking boots and her weatherproof jacket and headed out into the hills without a backward glance. But all that had changed once the children had arrived.

Pushing aside the uncomfortable thought that her life was posing some questions she didn't want to answer, she walked past him into the house. 'Perhaps we'll talk about it later.' She tossed her hair out of her eyes. 'When you eventually come back from the hospital.'

The atmosphere snapped tight between them

and Christy cursed herself. She hadn't intended to irritate or aggravate him. She'd wanted to be super-cool and indifferent in the same way that he was clearly indifferent to her.

If he wasn't indifferent, he would have followed her to London and talked about their problems.

He would have dragged her home where she belonged.

But he seemed to hurt her at every turn. Even now, by going straight back to the hospital, *by not wanting to be with her*, he was hurting her.

His eyes narrowed, his mouth tightened and his shoulders tensed. 'I'll take the cases up to your room.'

He sounded like a hotel concierge, Christy thought miserably as they trailed their way upstairs. Showing her around. Any minute now he'd be wishing her a pleasant stay. She'd expected anger and hostility, but what she hadn't expected was his coldness. She didn't know how to deal with coldness.

The children ran ahead, whooping and shrieking, excited about seeing their rooms again, oblivious of the rising tension between the two adults.

Envious of their carefree, uncomplicated approach to life, Christy watched them go. 'They're so pleased to be here,' she said softly, and Alessandro turned to her with something that was almost a growl.

'Of course they are pleased to be here. It's their home. They *never* should have left. And you never should have taken them!'

She inhaled sharply, shocked by the sharp stab of pain that lanced through her. He'd said that 'they' never should have left. He hadn't said anything about her. He didn't care about her. The only reason that he cared that she'd moved out was because he missed his children.

It was all about the children.

She felt a lump building in her throat and swallowed it down with an effort, reminding herself that she had to behave like an adult even though she wanted to break down and cry like a child.

'You're blaming me for this situation, Alessandro?'

'You're the one who decided to move out of the family home.'

It was only supposed to be temporary, she

wanted to shout. *You were supposed to come after me.* But pride stopped her saying what she wanted to say. Pride and the knowledge that he hadn't cared enough to come after her.

Her eyes blazed into his. 'And that makes this my fault?'

'I missed one lousy anniversary.' His eyes flashed dark with frustration and he ran both hands through his hair. 'And you walked out.'

Christy bit her lip. He just didn't get it. He couldn't even understand why she was so upset. How had they come to this?

She swallowed hard. 'It wasn't about the anniversary, Alessandro.' Although that had hurt badly. 'It was so much more than that. And we can't talk about this now. The children will hear us.'

'You didn't talk about it at any time,' he said roughly, his eyes dark and dangerous, his accent thicker than ever. 'You just left, ripping all the important things in my life away from me.'

She winced at his description and forgot her resolutions not to argue with him. 'I *tried* to talk to you but you were always at the hospital or out on a rescue!'

'It's my job, Christy.'

And he'd been avoiding the issue. 'We never communicate any more, Alessandro. When did you last spend time with me?'

'You were in my bed every single night.' His arrogant declaration brought a flush of colour to her pale cheeks.

'That was just sex,' she muttered. 'The only place we ever spent time together was in bed.'

Right from the first moment they'd met, they'd been unable to keep their hands off each other— to exercise anything even remotely resembling self-control.

Awareness throbbed between them and as she caught the passion and fire in his eyes, only partially concealed by thick, dark lashes. Painfully aware of his vibrant masculinity, she turned away, trying desperately to ignore the agony of need that flared inside her body.

It didn't mean anything, she told herself miserably. Alessandro was a red-blooded Mediterranean man and sex had always been important to him. It didn't mean that he loved her. Sex was not a way to solve problems.

But maybe it would be a start, she thought to herself.

If they shared a bed tonight, perhaps they'd feel closer and could start talking.

'When did we last spend time together, Alessandro?' she said in a choked voice. 'Wasn't I important? Do strangers in trouble matter more than your own wife?'

A muscle worked in his jaw and he let out a long breath, but before he could speak, the children came barrelling out of their bedrooms. 'We're going outside to play in the snow,' Katy yelled, ponytail flying as she took the stairs two at a time with Ben close behind her.

'Don't forget your coats,' Christy called after them, suddenly desperate for them to stay, to breathe life and fun into the place. She didn't want to be on her own with Alessandro. Didn't have the energy for the confrontation that was brewing.

Reading her mind, he took a step towards her. 'So—I'm here now. If you want to talk, then talk.' He looked remote and unapproachable and she felt everything sink inside her.

She knew that some of the nurses and junior

doctors found Alessandro intimidating, but she'd only ever loved the fact that he had no tolerance for anything less than perfection. It was what made him such an excellent doctor. So why did she suddenly find him so formidable?

'We can't talk about this in five minutes with you due back at the hospital. It's too important for that.'

'If you've got something to say, say it.' His mouth was grim as he moved towards her. 'You're trembling. Do I make you nervous, Christy?'

If he kissed her, she was lost.

She backed away and hated herself for it. 'Don't be ridiculous. Of course you don't make me nervous.'

'Feeling guilty about leaving?' He kept on coming, his eyes locked on hers. 'Conscience pricking you?'

'I don't have anything to feel guilty about.'

'Yes, you do.'

'You're seeing everything from one side as usual, which is totally unreasonable.'

'You talk to me about unreasonable when you were the one who walked out?'

There was a long silence while the atmosphere

throbbed and hummed. His dark eyes slid down to her mouth and she thought she saw a sudden flare of hunger. But then it was gone and he bent to pick up her case.

'You're right. This isn't the right time to talk about it. You've been gone for almost two months so waiting a few days longer for a cosy chat isn't going to kill either of us. I'll take this through to your room.' His tone was flat, emotionless and she watched him as he walked.

Her room? What did he mean, 'her room'?

Her knees still shaking, she followed him, her heart diving south as she saw that he'd put in her in the guest room. He stood for a moment, one dark eyebrow raised in challenge, and she bit her lip, hiding the pain.

So much for using sex as a problem-solver.

Was he expecting her to beg? Clearly he didn't want her sleeping in the same room as him, the same bed as him, but she wasn't going to let him know how much that hurt her. She had too much pride.

'Great. This is excellent.' She swept into the room as though the sleeping arrangements had been her choice. 'We did this up nicely, didn't we? I always liked the throw on the bed.'

His gaze was steady on her face. 'You should be comfortable enough.'

Oh, no, she wouldn't, she thought miserably. She wouldn't sleep a wink, knowing that he was just down the corridor. Sleeping naked... Alessandro always slept naked and she felt a sudden rush of heat at the thought. *She missed him so much.* 'I'll be fine. This is perfect.'

Something flamed in his dark eyes and she wondered what she'd said to anger him. After all, he'd been the one to put her in the spare room. If anyone had a right to be angry, surely it should be her? But he'd drawn the battle lines and made his position clear.

He didn't even want her in his bedroom. Didn't want their relationship to be mended.

And why did that come as a surprise? If he'd wanted to mend it, he would have followed her to London and dragged her back.

Which was what she'd thought he'd do.

She felt tears prick her eyes but fortunately Katy chose that moment to race back into the room, her hair and brightly coloured jumper dusted with snow. 'Oh, Mum, this is wicked. There's so much snow and—' She broke off and glanced around her. 'What are you doing in here?'

'This is where I'm sleeping, sweetheart.' Christy kept her tone bright, as if it were the most normal thing in the world for she and Alessandro to be sleeping apart, but Katy's expression changed from happy to stubborn.

'In the *spare room*?'

Christy suppressed a groan. Katy definitely saw too much. 'Your father and I need some space,' she said quietly, and Katy glowered at both of them.

'This is Christmas. Goodwill and all that. If you argue, you'll upset Ben.'

'We're not arguing,' Christy said weakly, and Alessandro gave a disapproving frown.

'Our sleeping arrangements are none of your business, Katherine.' He spoke quietly, but there was a warning note in his voice that made Katy's narrow shoulders tense.

'No.' Her expression was mutinous. 'You're not sleeping in here. I want you to sleep in the same bed, like everyone else's parents.'

'Sweetheart, plenty of your friends' parents don't sleep together. Look at Rosie's mum and dad. They—'

'That's different. They're divorced.' Katy glared at her fiercely. 'You and Dad are *not* getting divorced. That isn't going to happen.'

Christy heard Alessandro drag in a long breath and bit her lip hard. Just hearing the word said aloud made her feel sick but at that moment all her thoughts were channelled towards alleviating her daughter's distress.

'Look, sweetheart, you're too young to understand at the moment.' She kept her tone modulated and reasonable. 'But you have to leave this to Daddy and I. We'll sort it out together in our own way.'

Katy put her hands on her hips and gave an innocent smile. 'You think so?' And she turned on her heel and left the room.

Alessandro swore softly in Spanish. 'I will speak to her—'

'No.' Christy shook her head. 'She's upset. I'll talk to her later, when she's had time to calm down.'

'And what are you going to tell her? That this

was your choice? I need to get back to the hospital.' He gave her a long, burning look loaded with accusation and then strode out of the room. Christy stared after him, feeling numb. It was clear that he blamed her for the entire situation and the knowledge that he'd absolved himself of all responsibility should have stoked her anger. Instead, it left her feeling exhausted. She'd known Alessandro angry, she'd known him passionate but she'd never known him cold before now.

There was no hope for them. None at all.

And it promised to be anything but a happy and peaceful Christmas.

CHAPTER TWO

ALESSANDRO drove too fast, eyes narrowed, hands gripping the steering-wheel of his sports car.

He'd put her in the spare room, expecting to get a reaction, expecting her to throw herself into his arms. She hadn't even blinked.

Until she'd walked out three months earlier, they'd never even slept apart. Now she was behaving as though separate beds were an everyday occurrence.

Clearly it was what she wanted.

He parked in his space, still thinking about Christy, oblivious to the biting cold or the wail of approaching sirens.

She'd looked more beautiful than ever. She was the only woman he'd ever met who could appear so impossibly slender and yet still manage to have curves in all the right places. The gorgeous blue jumper had brought out the amazing colour of her eyes and her silky soft hair had tumbled past her shoulders like a blatant taunt. Had she done that on purpose? She knew how much he adored her hair. And then there were her legs, long, slim and tempting in those ridiculously high heels. She looked sexy and alluring and nothing like the way that a respectably married mother of two children was supposed to look.

Had she already taken another lover?

Discovering the meaning of insecurity for the first time in his life, Alessandro climbed out of the car, battling against a burning desire to put his fist through something. An ominous expression on his handsome face, he slammed his way through the doors that led from the ambulance bay into the department and almost crashed into his colleague.

'What are you doing here? We weren't expecting you back.' Sean Nicholson, the senior consultant in the A and E department and the leader of the mountain rescue team, took a step back, eyebrows raised in question.

Alessandro dragged in a breath and bottled up

his temper. 'We're short-staffed,' he said tightly. 'And this seems as good a place to be as any.'

Sean's eyes narrowed. 'That bad, eh?'

'Don't ask.'

'Doesn't do to run away from women,' Sean drawled. 'They catch up with you in the end.'

Only if they want to, Alessandro mused, his temper still stewing and simmering. Clearly Christy wanted no more to do with him. She'd moved out, come home only because she wanted the children to have a family Christmas, and she had no qualms about sleeping in the spare room.

Sean thrust a set on notes into his hand. 'Well, I'm not sorry you're here. This place is starting to resemble a war zone.'

A bit like home, then, Alessandro thought bitterly, walking through to a cubicle to see the patient that Sean had given him, but before he could open his mouth to speak, Sean caught his arm.

'Alessandro?' Sean's eyes were suddenly intent and thoughtful. 'I don't suppose Christy wants to come back to work, does she? Just for the two weeks leading up to Christmas? We've got six nurses off sick at the moment. The numbers just aren't adding up.'

'Christy?' Alessandro frowned. 'She's a practice nurse…'

Sean raised his eyebrows. 'Only for the last few years,' he said, his tone mild. 'Before that she was an A and E nurse, and a damn good one. I know it's a long shot, but…' He caught the dubious look on Alessandro's face and gave a shrug. 'Give it some thought.' He walked off and Alessandro stared after him.

It had been years since Christy had worked in A and E. She'd carried on working in the department part time after Katy's birth, but once Ben had arrived she'd given up completely for a few years and then taken a part-time job in the local GP practice.

Why would Sean think she could fill the gap in A and E? She'd be out of her depth, out of touch, unable to cope with the pressure—it was a ridiculous suggestion. Christy was a mother now. The children were her priority. There was no way she'd be able to cope with the demands of A and E.

He dismissed the thought instantly and buried himself in work. He worked through a long and busy night without taking a break and eventually arrived home at five in the morning.

The house was in darkness as he showered and crawled into his cold, empty bed. Sleep should have swallowed him whole but instead he stayed on the edges of wakefulness, unable to find the rest he craved.

His mind was full of Christy, at that moment probably sleeping peacefully in their spare bedroom.

The thought of her warm, perfect body sent his tension levels soaring and he eventually gave up on sleep just as the weak, winter light was filtering through the curtains. Cursing softly, his body thrumming with frustration, he pulled on a pair of fleecy tracksuit bottoms and a sweatshirt and went out for a run.

The snow was crisp and fresh on the ground, unmarked, and his breath clouded the air as he pounded silently along the track that led from his house to the river. Today the boulders were tipped with snow and the water was ice cold and as clear as glass. He ran until the breath tore at his lungs and his muscles ached and eventually arrived home to find the children sprawled on the sofas, watching Christmas cartoons on television. Christy was in the kitchen, making pancakes.

She glanced up as he walked into the room and for a moment they just stared at each other. Then she cleared her throat and turned back to the frying-pan, jiggling it with one hand to stop the pancake burning.

'Do you want some breakfast?' She was wearing a pair of jeans that fitted her snugly and the same blue jumper that he'd admired the day before. Her hair was loose, her cheeks were flushed and she looked pretty and far too young to be the mother of the two children watching television in the next room. Alessandro felt a vicious tug of lust that had him backing out of the room. It was just because he hadn't seen her for two months, he told himself firmly. As soon as he got used to having her around, he'd be able to control himself. Until then, he needed to keep some distance.

'No, thanks. No breakfast.' His stomach was

growling, the pancakes smelt delicious, but he couldn't trust himself to be in the same room as her and not grab her. Later, he promised himself, when he had his feelings well and truly under control, they'd talk. 'I need to get back to the hospital.'

'Alessandro.' Her voice was exasperated and she tilted her head to one side, her amazing, fiery hair sliding over her shoulder. 'You didn't come in until five and you were out running two hours after that. Even you need to rest some time!'

The only way she could possibly know the detail of his movements with such accuracy was if she hadn't been able to sleep either.

Registering that fact, he studied her face, saw the colour seep into her cheeks as she realised just how much she'd betrayed. Felt a flash of satisfaction that she wasn't as indifferent as she appeared to be. *Maybe there was hope for them.*

'Just for a few hours this morning,' he said huskily. 'We're ridiculously short-staffed. Everyone is off sick. I'll be back after lunch.' Suddenly he wished the children were at school so that he could just grab her and do what he wanted to do. He'd have her on the kitchen table in five seconds flat, naked in ten.

And he had a feeling that she wouldn't resist.

When had either of them ever been able to hold back in the bedroom? Their mutual passion had always been a driving force in their marriage. It was how they'd solved most of their problems.

'So short-staffed you're not even allowed to sleep?'

'There's a flu bug going around,' he muttered, dragging his eyes away from the smooth skin of her neck and trying to kill the erotic images dancing around his brain. 'Half the nurses are off sick.'

'You'll be joining them if you carry on pushing yourself like this,' she said tightly, and he sighed.

'You know what A and E is like.'

'Yes.' She grabbed some plates and slammed them down on the table with more force than was necessary. 'I should do. I used to work there and I was married to you for long enough.'

'Was?' He repeated the word, a jealous, possessive anger springing to life inside him. She must have detected something ominous in his tone because she looked up at him and he saw the misery in her eyes.

His insides twisted and he ran a hand over the back of his neck to relieve the growing tension. In all their years of marriage, he'd never seen Christy cry. He'd seen her helpless with laughter and wild with temper, but he'd never seen her cry and the shimmering mist of tears in her green eyes brought a sick feeling to the pit of his stomach.

'Christy—'

The phone rang and Christy leaned across to answer it, clearly relieved at the interruption.

Knowing her as he did, he guessed that such a display of weakness would have horrified her.

Alessandro watched as she pulled herself together. He heard her clear her throat and speak, saw a smile touch her wide, generous mouth and watched her glorious hair slide over her shoulder as she tilted her head and listened. He'd always loved her hair. The colour of autumn leaves, it fell past her shoulders in soft, wild curls. He was so absorbed by the soft, feminine curve of her jaw that he didn't even realise she'd replaced the receiver.

'That was Sean.'

'Nicholson?' Alessandro struggled to concentrate. 'Did he want to talk to me?'

'No.' Her voice was calm as she reached into the oven for the stack of pancakes she was keeping warm. 'He wanted to talk to me.'

'What about?'

Christy put the pancakes in the middle of the table. 'Working in A and E. He wants me to do bank work for the two weeks leading up to Christmas to cover all the nurses you have off sick.'

Alessandro watched while she reached into the fridge for maple syrup. 'And you said no.'

'Actually, I said yes.' She added a plate of lemon slices and a bowl of sugar to the table.

Alessandro stared at her in blatant astonishment. 'Why would you say yes?'

Her gaze lifted to his, her green eyes cool. 'Why wouldn't I?'

'Well, because…' He dragged a hand through his dark hair and frowned, suspecting that he was about to get himself into hot water. 'Because it's a long time since you've worked in A and E. You've been at home with the children for years now and—'

'And you think my brain has gone to mush?' Her tone had an edge to it as she reached into the cutlery drawer and withdrew a knife. 'Why don't you just say it, Alessandro? You don't think I'm up to it, do you?' She slammed the drawer shut with a decisive flick of her hand and Alessandro closed his eyes briefly and wished he'd stayed at the hospital.

'I'm just thinking of you. You've no idea what A and E is like now.' He spread lean, strong hands to emphasise his point. 'Every day there's a new piece of high-tech equipment to master and the work is full on and relentless. Every single day we're stretched to the limit. And then there's the violent drunks—'

She put the knife on the table next to the syrup. 'You don't think I can cope with a violent drunk?'

Alessandro eyed the dangerous glint in her eye and felt the hot burn of lust spread through his body. He'd always loved her passion and her strength. The fact that she was afraid of nothing. 'You're a strong woman, that's true, *querida*,' he drawled, 'but—'

'But nothing! Believe it or not, I still have a brain, Alessandro, and giving birth to your children hasn't changed that fact.' Passion and fire burned in her eyes and he was suddenly relieved that she'd put the knife down.

'You're overreacting.'

'Well, excuse me, but when I'm patronised I do have a tendency to overreact,' she said in a dangerously sweet tone. 'And let's be honest here for a moment, shall we? You're not thinking of me. You're thinking of yourself. You're afraid I'll embarrass you. Or that when you get home, your dinner won't be cooked. Or that I'll be too tired for sex—'

'Enough!' He said the word sharply, his eyes sliding to the door, but there was no sign of the children.

'Yes, Alessandro. I've had enough.' She glared at him. 'But you're not thinking of me, are you? You just don't want anything to upset the perfect order of your life.'

He inhaled sharply. 'A and E is busy and challenging and—'

'And you don't think I'm up to it,' Christy repeated, her jaw lifting in a stubborn expression that he knew so well. 'Well, I'm going to prove you wrong. I was a good nurse, Alessandro. You seem to have forgotten that.'

'I haven't forgotten that and you don't have to prove anything to me,' Alessandro said stiffly. 'You've been looking after the children and that's important. It's enough.'

'For you, yes. But what if it isn't enough for me?' Her voice was strangely flat. 'You carry on building your career, moving forwards and upwards, and you've never once stopped to wonder whether I'm happy standing still.'

Alessandro stared at her. 'I thought you were happy being at home with the children. Being a practice nurse.'

'Ben has been in full-time education for three years,' she replied shortly. 'And being a practice nurse was a forced decision based on the hours. You know that.'

Did he? *Did he know that?* Had he ever stopped to think about the choices she'd made? Feeling trapped in a corner, Alessandro ran a hand over the back of his neck.

'If you weren't happy, you should have talked to me.'

'When? The only way to guarantee an audience with you over the past year would have been to break something vital and arrive at your place of work in an ambulance.' She slammed a pan down on the side. 'I *tried* talking to you, Alessandro. You weren't listening.'

'I'm listening now.' He refrained from saying that he couldn't hear much above the banging and clattering that she was making as she worked her way around the kitchen.

She paused, the rapid rise and fall of her chest an indication of the depth of emotion bottled up inside her. 'And now isn't the time. Isn't that typical?' Rubbing a hand over her forehead, she gave a humourless laugh and took a breath. 'Children! Breakfast!'

Alessandro didn't budge from the doorway. 'We're going to talk about this, Christy.'

'Some time, yes, but the pancakes are getting cold so it can't be now.' She slid a pancake onto Ben's plate. 'But I'm starting at the hospital this afternoon. Late shift. You're looking after the children.'

Alessandro opened his mouth to suggest that

she delay it a few days to give him time to run through the essentials with her, but the children pushed past him and he decided that Christy was right. This wasn't the right time. She had no idea what A and E was like now, he thought fiercely, and made a mental note to ask Sean and Nicky to keep a discreet eye on her.

'You're working at the hospital, Mum?' Katy poured maple syrup over her pancakes. 'What's going to happen to us?'

'When Daddy isn't around, you'll go to Grandma's,' Christy said immediately, and Katy's face brightened.

'Cool. Shopping.'

Alessandro frowned. 'You don't mind spending most of the week at your grandmother's?'

'Why would I?' Katy gave a wide smile. 'She always says that the great thing about being a grandma is having someone to spoil. I'm more than happy to be that someone.'

'Her chocolate cake is awesome,' Ben added, heaping sugar in the middle of a pancake. 'It's all gooey and she cuts *really* big pieces. And she never worries about it spoiling your appetite.'

'You see?' Christy looked at Alessandro and gave a shrug. 'And, anyway, it will only be for part of the day. I'll still have plenty of time to spend with the children. Everyone's happy.'

Were they? Alessandro poured himself a strong cup of coffee and wondered what it would be like having Christy working in the department.

He was finding it hard enough being around her for the short period of time he was at home without contemplating falling over her at work, too.

'Look at it this way.' She gave him a smile loaded with subtle messages. 'You're always at the hospital. At least this way I get to see you.'

And that, Alessandro decided, was going to be the biggest problem. He wouldn't be able to use work to take his mind off Christy because she was going to be right there, under his nose.

'I can't believe you said yes to this.' Nicky, the A and E sister, grabbed Christy and gave her a hug. 'We are *so* pleased to see you back.'

'It's been years and I'm a bit nervous,' Christy confessed, stroking a hand down the blue scrub suit that the nurses wore in A and E. It felt unfamiliar. 'I'm afraid I'm going to make a mistake.'

'No way.' Nicky shook her head and waved a hand dismissively. 'You're an experienced nurse. And, anyway, if in doubt just shout.'

'Alessandro doesn't think I can do it,' Christy said softly, and Nicky gave her a searching look.

'Well, he's a traditional Mediterranean man but I guess you knew that when you married him. I suppose he sees you as his wife and the mother of his children. But that'll change after you've been in Resus together.'

Unless she messed it up. Christy felt a stab of insecurity. It was obvious that Alessandro thought she'd been away from A and E nursing for too long to be much use.

Would she be able to prove him wrong?

She, of all people, knew how exacting he was. He was noted for his absence of tolerance when it came to mistakes.

'Anyway, you've picked a good shift to start on,' Nicky said cheerfully, leading her round to the main area of the department. 'Your handsome husband isn't working this afternoon, so you can find your feet without him watching you with those brooding dark eyes. And it's Sunday afternoon. Lots of rugby injuries. Yummy men dressed in virtually nothing and covered in mud. My idea of heaven. Bring 'em on!'

Christy laughed, suddenly realising just how much she'd missed the camaraderie that was so much a part of working in the A and E department.

'Where do you want me to work this afternoon?'

'Out here at the sharp end,' Nicky said immediately. 'You can help me. It will be like old times. If it's quiet, we can warm our bottoms on the radiator and catch up on the gossip.'

Almost immediately the phone rang. Remembering that it was the hotline to Ambulance Control, Christy picked it up without hesitation, listening carefully while the person on the other end outlined the injuries of the patient they were bringing in.

When she'd replaced the receiver, she repeated the information to Nicky, her tone brisk and professional. 'Sounds bad. Shall I get Sean?'

'We need to assemble the trauma team,' Nicky agreed. 'Shame your Alessandro isn't on, it's right up his street. Still, never mind, we'll bleep the on-call orthopaedic reg.' Her eyes gleamed with humour. 'He'll have to do.'

The children were already asleep when she arrived home and Christy fell into bed, exhausted but elated. *She'd done it.* She'd worked a shift in A and E and she hadn't killed anyone or even slightly injured them. And she'd had fun. It had been exciting and unpredictable and the time had passed so fast that she'd been astonished when Nicky had pointed out that it was time to go home. Astonished and disappointed because she'd been enjoying herself. Really, really enjoying herself.

And now she was back in the spare bedroom. For a short time she'd forgotten about her problems. But there was no forgetting them now, with the cold, empty stretch of bed next to her.

He didn't want her, she reminded herself miserably.

He didn't want her in his bed and he didn't want her in his A and E department.

Leaving home and going to London had just

brought to a head something that would have happened anyway.

Their marriage was on a slow downhill slide and she didn't seem able to stop it.

The next morning, Christy scraped a thick layer of ice from her windscreen, dropped the children with her mother and arrived at A and E to find the department in chaos. The waiting room was full to bursting and the triage nurse looked unusually stressed as she tried to calm everyone and maintain order, filtering the urgent from the non-urgent.

'A bus carrying Father Christmas and a bunch of elves hit a patch of black ice at the head of the Kirkstone pass,' Nicky told her as she hurried past, carrying an armful of equipment. 'Mostly walking wounded but they've just brought the driver in and he's badly injured. Can you go into Resus and help? Alessandro is in there and they're short of a circulation nurse. Donna is there but she's newly qualified and I'm worried that your husband might take her head off if she's less than perfect. I need you to give her some help. I'm helping to stave off a riot out here. Apparently even elves don't respond well to four-hour waiting times.'

Without arguing or asking any further questions, Christy pushed open the doors of Resus and felt her heart hammer hard against her chest.

She hated to admit it, but the prospect of working with Alessandro made her nervous. She didn't need Nicky's reminder that he was capable of removing someone's head if he wasn't happy. It was one of the things she'd always respected about him. He cared deeply about each patient and wasn't willing to settle for anything other than best practice. She knew him to be an exacting taskmaster with a zero tolerance for anything other than perfection.

It was all very well for Nicky to tell her to keep an eye on Donna, but who was going to keep an eye on her?

What if she couldn't remember what to do?

A blood-stained Father Christmas outfit lay in a pile and the patient was groaning with pain. Alessandro stood at the head of the trolley, co-ordinating the medical team as he assessed the patient. 'There's some bruising over the anterior chest wall,' he murmured as his eyes slid over the patient, conducting a visual examination. 'No evidence of open wounds or penetrating trauma.'

Christy walked towards the trolley, momentarily distracted by the sight of him in action. She'd forgotten what an exceptionally gifted doctor he was. Slick, competent and a natural leader. Nothing ever fazed him.

He lifted his eyes from the patient and saw her. His expression didn't change. 'You need protective clothing before you handle the patient,' he said coldly. 'At the very least, latex gloves and an apron.' He turned his attention back to his patient and Christy felt the colour flood into her cheeks. Of course she knew that the first thing she should have done was to reach for protective clothing. All blood and body fluids had to be assumed to carry HIV and the hepatitis virus. She knew that. It was just that seeing him had rattled her. Affected her confidence.

Determined not to let him get to her, she quickly donned the clothing that she needed and walked back to the trolley.

Her hands were shaking and her heart was banging against her ribs. She'd done this before, she reminded herself firmly. Many times.

Alessandro was listening to the patient's chest, his face blank of expression as he concentrated. When he was satisfied, he looped the stethoscope round his neck and turned to the circulation doctor, a pretty blonde girl who was examining the patient's femur. 'Blood loss?'

'I'm keeping pressure on that wound and it's under control.'

'OK, I want two peripheral lines in and take some blood for cross-matching, full blood count, U and Es, and let's get an arterial sample. I want blood gas and pH analysis. What's his blood pressure doing? I need an ECG here.' His instructions were smooth and seamless and swiftly Christy took over from one of the other nurses, who was clearly struggling and whom she presumed to be Donna.

Instinctively her eyes flicked to the monitor as she reached for the adhesive electrode pads and attached the patient to the ECG monitor. 'It's dropping. Ninety over fifty.'

Suddenly her hands weren't shaking any more. Her movements were smooth, confident and almost automatic. She knew what she was doing and it was as if she'd never been away.

'We'll start with a litre of Hartmann's,' Alessandro said immediately, and Christy busied herself with her patient while he made a rapid assessment of brain and spinal-cord function.

'Put your tongue out for me,' he instructed the patient. 'Wiggle your toes.'

'His blood pressure is still dropping,' Christy said quietly, and Alessandro's gaze flickered to hers.

'Increase the flow rate and let's give him some analgesia.'

'First line is in,' the blonde doctor said as she slid a wide-bore cannula into a vein and Christy pulled the IV stand towards her so that she could attach the giving set and start the infusion.

'Get that second line in straight away, Katya,' Alessandro instructed, and the blonde doctor reached for the second cannula and moved round the trolley to the other side of the patient.

The man gave a groan of pain and Alessandro

immediately switched his attention back to his patient. 'We're going to give you something for the pain now, Derek,' he said calmly and Christy reached for the drugs that she knew would be on the trolley. 'Morphine and cyclizine?'

With speed and efficiency she drew up the drug and handed it to Alessandro, along with the ampoule to check. Then she moved closer to the trolley and closed her hand over the patient's, offering comfort.

'We'll soon have you more comfortable, Derek,' she said quietly, and felt the man's fingers tighten over hers.

This was the bit that the doctors often forgot or ignored, she thought to herself as she felt the man's grip. They forgot the importance of touch. They forgot that as well as being injured, the patient was anxious and scared.

It was another thing that she'd always admired about Alessandro. No matter how tense the situation, he never forgot his patient. He wasn't a touchy-feely doctor, but he understood the importance of communication in lowering stress levels.

Her eyes flickered to the machines next to her.

'His blood pressure is stable,' she said quietly, and Alessandro gave a nod.

'Good. He's still in pain so I'm going to give him a femoral nerve block before we splint and X-ray.'

Immediately Christy reached for the needle she knew he was going to need and an ampoule of lignocaine.

Alessandro felt for the femoral artery and cleaned the skin. Then he held out his hand for the local anaesthetic that Christy had prepared.

She watched while he inserted the needle perpendicular to the skin and then aspirated to check for blood. 'That's fine,' he murmured, moving the needle up and down as he injected the local anaesthetic.

Katya moved forward, standing close to Alessandro. 'What happens if you puncture the artery?'

'I resign.' Sounding impossibly Spanish, Alessandro dropped the syringe back on the tray that Christy was holding and gave a brief smile. 'But before I resign, I compress it for five to ten minutes or until the bleeding stops. Then I carry on with the femoral nerve block.' He turned his attention back to his patient. 'That should give you some relief very quickly, Derek.'

Katya turned away but not before Christy had seen the flirtatious glance.

She wanted Alessandro.

Christy's stomach lurched and she swallowed hard.

She was used to women staring at Alessandro. It had always happened and perhaps it always would because he was a man who inevitably attracted the attention of the female sex. But this was the first time she'd seen it happen when their marriage was in trouble.

Had he done something about it?

She bit her lip. Katya was very pretty. Alessandro was a hot-blooded Spaniard with a high sex drive, she knew that better than anyone. With their marriage in its current state, it was hard not to worry.

Had something happened between them?

The man closed his eyes and shook his head. 'We were on our way to a school—delivering presents.'

'Don't worry about that now.' Pushing aside

disturbing thoughts of Katya with her arms wrapped around Alessandro, Christy gave a reassuring smile as the man gripped her hand tightly.

'Will you get someone to phone the school and explain? These kids believe in Father Christmas. What will they think if I don't turn up?'

Alessandro looked taken aback but Christy squeezed the man's hand. 'I'll talk to one of the nurses outside see if one of your elves can make a call.'

Alessandro looked at her blankly and she just smiled and turned to Donna, who was hovering nervously. 'Can you speak to Nicky?' she said quietly. 'Ask her to talk to one of the elves and call the school.'

Visibly relieved to be given an excuse to leave, Donna backed out of the room.

Alessandro watched her go with an ominous frown in his dark eyes. 'She's nervous.'

'She's learning and you can be scary,' Christy said calmly. 'Do you want to immobilise the limb now?'

He looked at her. 'I'm scary?'

'Not everyone is born with your confidence.

Derek, we're going to splint this leg of yours and for that I need to take some measurements on your uninjured leg.' Having offered an explanation, Christy moved the blanket and measured the uppermost part of the patient's thigh.

Donna slipped back by her side. 'It's done,' she said breathlessly. 'They've phoned the school and everyone is fine.'

'Good. Well done.' Christy smiled at her patient. 'You can stop worrying. Even Father Christmas is allowed to be held up when he's delivering presents.'

He smiled weakly. 'You probably think I'm mad, worrying about that while I'm lying here with a broken leg, but I don't want to disappoint the children. I think the pain is getting easier.'

'The splint will help the pain, too,' Christy explained, and then turned to Donna and handed her the measurements she'd taken. 'We're going to use a Thomas splint. Can you go and fetch me one, please? You'd better get the size above and below, just in case. It will save you making another journey.'

Working as a team, they prepared to fit the

splint and Christy applied the adhesive tape and then wrapped the leg from ankle to mid-thigh with gauze bandage, talking Donna through what she was doing.

The girl lost her nervous appearance and moved closer to the trolley, her expression keen and interested.

Alessandro applied traction to the leg, gently pulling the ankle with one hand and supporting the knee with the other.

Katya stood closer to him than was strictly necessary and Christy tried not to mind and concentrated instead on helping Donna.

'You can see that he's correcting the abduction and the external rotation,' she explained as she helped manoeuvre the splint onto the leg until it was in the right position.

She and Alessandro worked together smoothly, closely observed by both Katya and Donna.

Once the cords were tied and twisted, Christy put wool roll padding under the thigh. 'Now we just need to bandage the whole splint from thigh to lower calf,' she said to Donna, 'lift and support the leg on a pillow and check the distal pulses.'

'Great.' Alessandro turned to Katya. 'Can you arrange for X-rays and then we'll refer him to the orthopaedic team? I want X-rays of the pelvis, hip and knee.'

Katya gave a feline smile. 'Of course, Alessandro.'

Donna shot a questioning glance at Christy, who dragged her gaze away from her scrutiny of Katya and volunteered the information she knew was needed.

'For the femoral shaft to fracture, there must have been a violent high-energy impact and that is associated with other injures.' *He wouldn't be sleeping with Katya*, she told herself firmly. *Alessandro wouldn't do that.* He might be the archetypal alpha male, but he was an honourable man with strong principles. 'So when we're X-raying, it's important to check pelvis, hip and knee.'

But if he considered their marriage to be over, would he do that?

CHAPTER THREE

CHRISTY started to clear up some of the debris that had accumulated while Katya and Donna arranged the X-rays. She knew how important it was to keep Resus tidy and well stocked, and she thought that the comfort of routine might relieve the sick feeling building in her stomach.

Forcing herself to be rational and mature, she hung a fresh bag of IV fluid from the drip stand and then started to replenish the drugs that they'd used.

Eventually the patient was transferred to Theatre and she was left alone in the room. She picked up a laryngoscope from the intubation tray and snapped it open, testing that the bulb worked. She stared down at the curved, silver blade in her hand and didn't hear the door open behind her.

'So—working in A and E is obviously like riding a bike.' Alessandro's deep, masculine drawl came from directly behind her and she turned, her stomach jumping. There was no reason to feel nervous, she told herself firmly. They'd worked together as a smooth, efficient team. She hadn't done anything wrong.

'It came back to me.'

'Obviously.' His dark eyes lingered on her face. 'You've missed it, haven't you?'

She caught her breath. It had been years since she'd stopped working in A and E and yet that was the first time he'd ever asked her that question. 'Yes,' she breathed. 'I missed it terribly.'

Something flickered in his eyes. 'You never said.'

'You never asked.'

Their eyes met and held and Christy felt the heat flicker and stir in her pelvis.

Why did she have to find him so completely irresistible? The attraction between them was so powerful that it blinded her to every other aspect of their relationship, which was probably the reason they hadn't sorted their problems out earlier.

'We should talk more,' he said roughly, and she gave a wan smile.

'You're not always that easy to talk to, Alessandro.'

'Am I really scary?' There was a frown in his eyes and she realised that her earlier comment had genuinely bothered him.

'You can be intimidating,' she said honestly. 'But that's partly because of your skills and experience. You can't expect a newly qualified nurse to respond to an emergency situation with your confidence.'

'If she can't cope with the situation, she shouldn't be in Resus,' Alessandro growled, and Christy sighed.

'You're so hard on people. In an ideal world, I suppose you're right. But we don't live or work in an ideal world. And the best way to learn is by the patient's bedside, gaining hands-on experience with the appropriate supervision.' She scanned the trolley, checking that she'd replaced all the drugs they'd used. 'All the studying in the world doesn't prepare you for the pressure and demands of Resus when a patient is bleeding before your eyes.'

Alessandro looked at her thoughtfully. 'You were good with her,' he conceded. 'The nurse, I mean.'

It was so unlike him to offer praise that she blinked in astonishment and then felt the warmth spread inside her.

'Thank you.'

'Do I scare *you*?' His direct question made her catch her breath.

She wondered whether she ought to admit that the only thing that scared her was the thought of losing him.

She opened her mouth to tell him, but pride trapped the words in her throat before she could utter them. *She was sleeping in the spare room*, she reminded herself. *He hadn't come after her.*

It was the wrong time to be honest about her feelings when she was so unsure about his.

'No,' she said finally, her voice quiet. 'You don't scare me, but you can be difficult to reach and sometimes I just give up rather than keep trying.'

He muttered something in Spanish and ran a hand over his jaw, a jaw that was already showing signs of stubble. Then he reached out and slid a hand behind her head and pulled her face to within inches of his in a gesture that was both male and possessive. 'I *don't* want a divorce, Christy. Be clear about that.'

She stared up at him, hypnotised by the look in his dark, brooding eyes. They were the words she'd waited to hear for two long months and he'd chosen to say them in Resus under harsh, fluorescent lights with the likelihood that they'd be disturbed at any moment. She wanted to ask why he'd let her go. She wanted to ask about Katya. Suddenly, she wanted to know how he'd spent the last six weeks. 'And what if I want a divorce?'

She said the words to goad him and remembered too late that goading Alessandro, with his volatile, Latin temperament, was not a good idea.

'You don't.' He slid his other arm and around her and jerked her against him in a decisive gesture that was so much a part of him.

She felt the strength and power of his body and the breath trapped in her throat. 'Alessandro…' she couldn't concentrate on anything when he was this close. Couldn't think…

'Need me to prove it to you?' He breathed the words against her mouth, his tone silky smooth and dangerous, and she gave a whimper, knowing what was coming and willing herself to reject him. 'Need me to prove that you still want me?'

'No, I don't, I—'

His mouth came down on hers with seductive intent and immediately she sank against him because no one kissed like Alessandro and resisting him was impossible. His hand was buried in her hair, the skilful slide of his tongue erotic and demanding as he took her to the edge of sanity with a speed that shocked her.

His kiss was hungry and primitive and she clutched at him, pressing against him, her need so intense that she forgot everything except her desire for him.

Kissing him gave her the reassurance she needed and then he released her and stepped back, his expression cold. 'The children need both their parents. We're a family, Christy, and that isn't going to change.'

The tiny flicker of hope died inside her. 'Alessandro—'

'We won't ever speak of divorce again, Christy. And don't pretend you don't want me.'

Oh, she wanted him. How could she pretend

otherwise when her nipples were pressing hard against the soft fabric of her scrub suit and her mouth was still swollen from the ravages of his kiss?

She wanted him. But how did she explain that she needed more than the physical when his solution to every problem was sex? He was a red-blooded, Mediterranean male with a high sex drive. She'd known that right from the first. *Had loved the fact that he couldn't get enough of her.*

And the fact that he'd made it clear that his thoughts were only for the children caused her intense pain. The kiss hadn't been about her, she thought miserably. It had been about the children. Alessandro was Spanish, through and through. He believed utterly in the sanctity of the family.

He would stay married to her for the sake of the children.

Could she do the same? Could she stay with him, knowing that he didn't love her any more?

'We can't talk about this here, Alessandro,' she croaked. 'Not now.'

His eyes dropped to her mouth and the tension rose between them.

'When, then?'

'I don't know.' She felt so shaky and miserable that she didn't feel up to another confrontation. Didn't feel up to listening to more evidence that he was determined to save their marriage for the sake of the children.

'Well, it has to be soon.' He was standing close to her. So close that her heart rate increased alarmingly.

Was it normal? she wondered. Was it normal to be married to someone for twelve years and yet still want to rip their clothes off at every opportunity?

'I need to go home and prepare dinner,' she said huskily as she dragged off her gloves and washed her hands, seeking any excuse to turn away from him. 'Mum's dropping the children in an hour. Are you joining us?'

She expected him to tell her that he was staying at the hospital but as she risked a glance at him she collided with his hard, unyielding gaze.

'*Sí.*' His Spanish accent was more pronounced than usual. 'I'm joining you, *querida*. I want to eat dinner with my children. Why wouldn't I?'

The children.

It was all about the children, she thought dully as she washed her hands and walked out of the room.

As a couple, they didn't exist any more.

Checking that her parents were still seated at the dining table, Katy grabbed her brother's hand and dragged him upstairs and into the spare bedroom. 'It's time to interfere.'

'What's interfere?' Ben started playing with his toy aeroplane and Katy snatched it away from him and held it out of reach.

'Interfere is when you try and help someone do something they should be doing for themselves.' She threw the aeroplane onto a chair and grabbed his hand. 'Come on. We're going to bounce on the bed.'

Ben tried to jerk his hand away from hers. 'I was playing with my aeroplane.'

Katy rolled her eyes. 'You can play with it again in a minute, but for now we're going to bounce.'

Ben eyed the bed doubtfully. 'We're not supposed to jump on the beds.'

'And when has that ever stopped you?'

'I'll get into trouble with Mum.'

'And if you don't do it, you'll get into trouble with me,' Katy informed him sweetly. 'Take your pick.'

'I do like bouncing.' Ben looked at the wide bed with something close to yearning. 'Come on, then. Just a quick one. How hard do you want me to bounce?'

'Just hard enough to break it,' Katy muttered under her breath, slipping off her shoes. 'I'll help you. Come on.' And she leapt into the middle of the bed and started jumping, her dark ponytail flying around her shoulders as she leaped higher and higher.

Ben gave a delighted giggled and climbed up next to her.

'Come on.' She grabbed his hands and encouraged him to bounce, too.

Downstairs in the kitchen, Christy and Alessandro were finishing their meal in tense silence when there was an enormous crash above them, followed by a plaintive yell.

'Oh, no.' Driven by her maternal instincts,

Christy was out of her seat and up the stairs in record time, Alessandro right behind her.

In the bedroom they found Ben sobbing noisily on the carpet and Katy with her arms around him. She looked up when her parents entered. 'Poor Ben. He bounced on the bed and...' she gave a baffled shrug, her expression both innocent and mystified '...it must have broken or something. Unbelievable, the rubbish they sell you these days.'

'The bed broke?' Christy looked at the collapsed bed in horror and disbelief. 'Oh, my goodness. It looks as though the frame has snapped right through. How did you—?' And then she saw the blood on Ben's cheek and dropped to her knees. All the training in the world didn't prepare you properly for coping when your own child was injured, she thought frantically. 'You're bleeding. Alessandro, he's bleeding.'

'I see it.' Calm and steady, Alessandro scooped his son into his arms and swept the aeroplane and Christy's clothes off the chair so that he could sit down. 'What's happened to you?'

'Katy told me to bounce,' Ben hiccoughed, his

face blotched with crying, 'so I bounced, but when the bed broke I fell off and banged myself. It hurts.'

'Where did you bang yourself?' Alessandro ran strong fingers over the little boy's arms and legs, hunting for damage—trying to find the source of the bleeding. He found it on the boy's palm. 'It's fine. Just a scratch. He must have run his hand over his cheek. That's why he has blood on his face.'

Christy stood there, heart thumping, relieved that Alessandro was there. She'd always been a wreck inside when either of the children had been ill or injured. She suddenly realised how much she'd missed his strength.

Still cuddling Ben, Alessandro threw a frowning glance at the bed. 'That's well and truly broken. You won't be sleeping there tonight.'

Christy gave a tiny frown and turned to Katy. 'I'll have Ben's room. Your brother can share with you.'

'No way!' Katy shrank back, her face a picture of exaggerated sibling horror. 'He snores, fidgets and talks in his sleep. No way am I sleeping with a monster baby like him.'

Ben clutched at the front of Alessandro's shirt and scowled at his sister. 'I'm *not* a baby!'

Christy sighed. 'Katy, there's no other option.'

'Yes, there is. If there's sharing to be done, you can jolly well share with Dad. At least you're married. I'm *not* sharing with my brother! That's totally gross.' And she stomped out of the room, ponytail swishing like a statement.

Alessandro stared after her with an expression of blatant masculine incomprehension. 'Is she hormonal?'

Christy rubbed her aching forehead. 'Hardly. She's eleven years old.'

'She's acting like a teenager.'

'She's going through a difficult phase. She's…' Her eyes met his and the words tailed off. They both knew that if Katy was going through a difficult stage, it was probably their fault. Christy's hand fell to her side. 'On top of everything else, I suppose it isn't exactly fair for her to have to share with her brother. She is getting to an age where privacy is important,' she murmured, and Alessandro nodded agreement.

'You can use our bedroom. I'll take the sofa downstairs.'

Christy felt the heavy punch of disappointment deep inside her but smiled. 'That's very decent of you. Thanks.'

She didn't care, she told herself. She didn't care that he obviously couldn't face the thought of sharing a room with her, let alone a bed. *She didn't care that he'd rather sleep on the sofa than be with her.*

Once, they hadn't been able to keep their hands off each other. They'd been like greedy, naughty teenagers seizing every opportunity to rip each other's clothes off and feast. Now it seemed as if they couldn't create enough distance.

'How will Father Christmas come if Daddy's sleeping downstairs?' Ben's anxious voice interrupted her thoughts. 'We all know that he can't come if anyone is there to see him.' The sweet innocence of his question made her heart twist.

'I…er… He…' Christy fumbled for an answer that might work, casting a desperate look at Alessandro.

'I'll keep my eyes tightly shut for the whole night?'

Ben shook his head, his expression solemn. 'That won't work. If you're awake, he knows.'

'Well, Daddy's under a lot of strain at the moment,' Alessandro growled, 'so I'm sure I'll be asleep.'

Was he under strain? He always looked infuriatingly cool and relaxed, Christy mused as she studied his handsome face for clues. Perhaps those dark, brooding eyes were a little more shadowed than usual and the sexy mouth a little more grimly set.

The strain of having her to stay, she thought miserably.

He was only tolerating her because of the children. Everything he did was because of the children.

'That's settled, then,' Christy said brightly. 'Daddy will sleep on the sofa. Now, let's get you into bed. It's getting late.'

She woke early to the sound of clattering and thumping in the kitchen, accompanied by harsh masculine curses. Trying to ignore the fact that she'd had less than four hours' sleep, she slipped on her dressing-gown and went downstairs to investigate.

Bare-chested and wearing only a pair of old jeans, Alessandro was muttering to himself in Spanish as he smashed his way around the kitchen.

Her Spanish was by no means fluent, but she'd lived with him for long enough to understand that he was in a foul temper.

'What's the matter with you?'

Alessandro shot her a stormy look as he made himself a large espresso. 'It's morning. I hate mornings. Especially after a night spent in the equivalent of a shoebox.'

She tried not to look at that tempting expanse of muscular chest. He had an incredible physique. Hard. Strong. Male. 'That sofa was expensive.'

He made a sound that was close to a snarl. 'Believe me, you'd never guess by sleeping on it. I'm aching in parts of my body that I never even knew I had before now.'

He looked so cross that she felt a smile coming and lifted a hand to her mouth to cover it.

He paused with the cup halfway to his lips, his smouldering gaze hooded. 'Are you laughing at me?' He rolled the 'r', sounding more and more Spanish as he always did when he was angry.

'I'm not laughing at you.'

Slowly, he placed the cup back on the work surface, his eyes glittering dark and dangerous as he moved purposefully towards her. 'Because if you're laughing at me, *querida*, *you* can spend the night on the sofa tonight.'

Her heart started to thump hard against her ribs and she found herself backing away. 'Alessandro, I wasn't laughing.' It was ridiculous that he could still have this effect on her, she told herself firmly. They'd been together for twelve years. It wasn't possible for a man to make a woman weak at the knees after twelve years. It didn't happen that way. People became bored with each other. Sex was supposed to become routine and infrequent.

'You would fit better on the sofa.' He was right up against her now, and she was right up against the wall. Breathing heavily. 'You are smaller. More delicate.'

At that particular point in time she didn't need him to point out their differences. Her eyes were in line with sleek, male muscle and dark body hair. He was pumped up and hard and breathtakingly sexy. There was certainly no missing the differences between them.

'I'll sleep on the sofa if that's what you want.' Why did he persist in standing so close to her? What was he thinking?

And then she made the mistake of lifting her eyes to his and instantly knew exactly what he was thinking. He was thinking of sex. She recognised the sudden darkening of his eyes, saw the tiny pulse flicker in his rough jaw. He hadn't shaved yet and he looked more like a bandit than a senior doctor loaded with responsibilities.

Her tongue flickered out in what was actually a nervous gesture, but his eyes dropped to her mouth and she sensed the change in him.

He lifted a hand and brushed her cheek gently, his breathing unsteady. 'Christy…'

He was going to kiss her.

She closed her eyes, her blood thundering round her body in excited anticipation, and then there was a clatter and laughter as the two children surged into the room.

Alessandro cursed softly and backed away from her, retreating to his abandoned coffee-cup and leaving Christy ready to sob with frustration.

'Hi, Mum.' Katy dragged a chair away from the table and sat down with one leg curled underneath her. 'Dad. Good night?'

'Marvellous. Perhaps you would like to bounce on the sofa as well as the bed,' Alessandro suggested with sarcastic bite, 'and then I wouldn't have to sleep on it.'

Ben frowned, puzzled as he poured milk into his cup, slopping it everywhere. 'But you don't like us bouncing on the furniture.'

'Dad was joking,' Katy said calmly, reaching for a cloth to mop up the mess her brother had made. 'He's obviously in a bad mood because he slept badly. Tonight he'd better sleep in the bed.'

Alessandro threw his daughter an exasperated

look and then turned to Christy. 'How does she suddenly know so much?'

Christy gave a weak smile. 'She's growing up. Don't worry. I'll sleep on the sofa tonight. We'll take turns.'

She poured herself another cup of coffee and missed the thoughtful smile on her daughter's face.

The first person she saw when she arrived at work was Jake Blackwell, the obstetrician.

'Babe! I heard you were back.' He strolled towards her and dragged her into his arms for a hug.

Christy closed her eyes and held onto him. He was their oldest friend and suddenly she wondered exactly what Alessandro had told him. 'It's good to see you.'

Jake gently disengaged himself and looked down at her with a searching gaze. 'That bad, huh?'

'Oh, no, everything is fine,' she lied with a forced smile, and Jake gave a soft laugh.

'If everything is fine, my angel, then why is Alessandro taking everyone's heads off and walking round like a volcano on the brink of eruption?'

'He's angry with me because I took the children away,' Christy muttered, and Jake looked at her thoughtfully.

'You think so?'

Christy stepped back and ran a hand through her hair to check it was still in place. 'What other reason would there be?'

Jake's eyes narrowed. 'Well, I can think of another one but this probably isn't the time or the place to go into that. Are you going to offer to cook me dinner some time? Don't forget I'm just a poor, starving bachelor and I haven't had one of your meals for weeks.'

Christy smiled. It was so good to have friends, she reflected. 'Of course.' It would make eating with Alessandro less tense. 'Are you dating someone special at the moment?'

Jake gave her a wicked smile. 'You know me, still auditioning for Miss Right.'

Christy sighed. She did know him. Knew his fearsome reputation with women. 'You should settle down, Jake.'

'When I find the love of my life, I'll settle down,' he drawled, 'and not a moment before. I have you and Alessandro as an example.'

'Us?' She looked at him, startled. 'What sort of an example are we?'

'The very best,' Jake said softly, lifting a hand to her cheek. 'And don't you forget that. You're crazy about each other.'

'We're separated.'

'So?' Jake gave a dismissive shrug. 'You're both passionate, fiery people. You've lost your way for a while but you'll find it again.'

No, they wouldn't.

She'd lost hope.

Suddenly Christy wanted to blurt everything out. She wanted to tell Jake that Alessandro had put her in the spare room and that he wasn't interested in her any more, but she couldn't do that standing in a draughty, hospital corridor.

As if to confirm that point, Jake's bleeper suddenly sounded and he lifted it from his pocket and read the number with a rueful smile. 'Here we go again. Women just can't do without me.'

Christy couldn't help the smile. 'You haven't changed.'

'And neither have you and Alessandro.' He put the bleeper back in his pocket and gave her a thoughtful look. 'Remember that, Christy. I'll see you later.'

She watched him go, knowing that he was wrong. She *had* changed. Probably more than she'd realised.

'Christy?' Nicky appeared in the corridor. 'I've got a woman coming in by ambulance who collapsed on the tennis court. Can you deal with her?'

Christy hurried towards her. 'Tennis? There's snow on the ground.'

'Indoor court.' Nicky grinned and pushed her into Resus. 'She's on her way now. Billy can help you to start with and he can call Alessandro if he needs to. We don't really know how serious it is. Her sister is following by car. I'll put her in the relatives' room with a cup of tea but don't forget to update her when you have some news.'

The woman arrived still dressed in her white tennis gear and clutching a vomit bowl.

'This is Susan Wilde. She was very sick in the

ambulance,' the paramedic said as they lifted her from their stretcher onto the trolley. 'She was playing tennis when she suddenly complained of a headache and collapsed.'

Christy covered the woman with a blanket while she listened to the handover and then Billy arrived and started his examination.

'Mrs Wilde? Can you remember what happened?'

The woman turned her head slowly and looked at him blankly, as if she was having trouble focusing and concentrating. 'Don't know… Pain…' She groaned. 'Neck, head.' Her eyes drifted shut again and Christy checked her observations quickly.

'Her pulse is down and her BP is up,' she said quietly. 'I'll get you a venflon so that you can put a line in and we'll give her some oxygen straight away.'

Billy stared at her and then nodded. 'OK. Yes. Good idea.' He ran a hand through his hair and let out a breath. 'I might just give Mr Garcia a call. Ask him to take a look at her.'

'You get a line in and I'll call him for you,'

Christy advised, handing him the necessary gear and then attaching ECG electrodes to the patient's chest. 'He's going to want you to have obtained venous access. It looks as though she might have had a subarachnoid haemorrhage.'

'Right.' Taking the tourniquet from the tray she'd handed him, Billy slid it onto the patient's arm and pulled it tight. As he searched for a vein and slid the venflon into place, Alessandro walked into the room.

'Everything all right in here?'

'I was just going to come and ask your advice,' Billy confessed, releasing the tourniquet and raising his eyebrows as Christy handed him a selection of bottles. 'What are those for?'

'BMG, FBC, clotting screen and U and Es,' Christy said calmly, reaching for the forms to go with the bottles and filling out all of them except the doctor's signature. 'I'll just go and arrange for a chest X-ray because it's obvious that you're going to need one of those.'

She thought she saw a flicker of amusement

and admiration in Alessandro's eyes as she walked towards the phone.

By the time she'd finished, Alessandro was examining the patient, who by now was so drowsy she could barely answer and was making little sense at all.

Christy was just wondering whether the woman had actually lapsed into unconsciousness when she gave another groan, rolled onto her side and vomited weakly.

Christy got the bowl there in time and Alessandro frowned.

'We need to give her some morphine and an anti-emetic. Christy, I want you to arrange an urgent CT scan and contact the neurosurgeons.'

'I've already arranged the scan and the neurosurgeons are on their way down.' Christy drew up the drugs that he'd requested and gave them to him to check while Billy stared in amazement.

'You called the scanning department already? When did you arrange that?'

'At the same time that I arranged the chest X-ray. It seemed sensible.' Christy checked the woman's observations on the monitor. 'She's showing signs of raised intracranial pressure, do you want to give her some IV mannitol?'

'We'll do the scan straight away and discuss it with the neurosurgeons,' Alessandro said, a strange light in his eyes as he looked at her. 'I'd forgotten what it was like to work with you.'

She gave him a cool look. 'Had you?' He thought of her as the mother of his children, she realised suddenly. He didn't really see her as an individual any more.

Didn't think she was a capable nurse.

'Is there anything else you need?' she asked. 'Because her sister is in the waiting room and she needs an update. I can send Donna through to help you here and go with her to the scanner.'

'Go and talk to the sister,' Alessandro said immediately, 'and tell her I'll be able to tell her more once we've done the scan and talked to the neurosurgeons.'

Christy pulled off her apron, washed her hands and then walked towards the relatives' room.

CHAPTER FOUR

'So what's it like having your wife under your nose in the department,' Jake asked cheerfully as he piled butter onto a baked potato and dropped two bars of chocolate on his tray.

'Surprisingly good. At least she knows what she's doing, which is more than can be said for half the people I'm expected to work with at the moment.' Alessandro eyed Jake's tray with disbelief as they stood in the queue, waiting to pay. 'Blackwell, you do realise that the contents of your tray are likely to give you a heart attack before morning?'

Jake shrugged. 'Chocolate and baked potatoes are the only edible objects in this restaurant. And I don't see why you're surprised about Christy. She was always a brilliant nurse. The brightest I ever worked with.'

'I forgot you worked with her.'

'She did an obstetrics module. All the doctors were crazy about her.'

Alessandro scowled. 'I didn't need to hear that.'

'Why not? It's the truth.' Jake studied a cake loaded with cream. 'Christy is gorgeous.'

'You're talking about the mother of my children,' Alessandro said coldly, and Jake shrugged and walked past the cake.

'So? That doesn't stop her being gorgeous. And, anyway, I thought you didn't want her any more.'

Alessandro inhaled sharply. 'Who said I didn't want her any more?'

'You didn't follow her to London.'

'She left to get away from me,' Alessandro said grittily. 'I assumed that following her would inflame the situation.'

'Did you?' Jake shot him a curious look. 'You really don't understand women at all, do you?'

Alessandro stared at his friend with mounting irritation. 'And you do?'

'Of course. I'm an obstetrician. I'm paid to understand women.' They arrived at the till and

Jake beamed at the plump, smiling woman who looked at his tray and clucked with disapproval.

'Where's the nutrition in that lunch, Dr Blackwell?'

'I need energy, not nutrition, Delia,' Jake said cheerfully. 'We're busy on the labour ward and I'm going to need more than carrots to see me through until midnight. That's a nice jumper. The colour suits you. Is it new?'

'You always notice the little things.' Delia beamed and handed him his change. 'Early Christmas present from my daughter who lives in Canada.'

'Is that Gillian? The one with the two-year-old?'

Delia blushed with delight. 'Is there anything you don't remember, Jake?'

'I'm programmed to remember the details of everyone's labour and delivery,' Jake responded with a cheerful wink as he pocketed the change and lifted his tray.

Alessandro rolled his eyes as they walked to the nearest vacant table. 'Do you have to flirt with every woman you meet?'

'Yes, I think I probably do.' Jake sat down and

picked up his fork. 'Believe it or not, Garcia, women like it when you notice them. You ought to drop your intimidating Mediterranean macho act and try it some time. Having a guy who behaves like a caveman might be a woman's fantasy, but when it comes to reality they want a man to talk to them.'

Alessandro bit into his sandwich with more savagery than was strictly necessary. 'What are you implying?'

'Nothing.'

Alessandro put the sandwich down on his plate. 'You're suggesting that I don't talk to Christy, but she was in London before I realised anything was wrong and now she's back I can't seem to reach her.'

'No.' Jake dug his fork into the potato and gave him a bland smile. 'Of course you can't.'

'Did you think Christy was happy being a practice nurse?'

Jake chewed thoughtfully. 'Well, she liked the hours, of course, because it meant that she could always be there for the children.' He waved his fork. 'But she missed the pace of A and E. Hardly surprising, really. I think she quite liked things like the asthma clinic because she could make quite a difference to the patients' lives, but syringing ears and doing dressings drove her nuts.'

Alessandro stared at him. 'When did she tell you all that?'

'I don't know.' Jake pushed his plate away and reached for his first bar of chocolate. 'We've chatted about it over the years. Christy was quite a high-powered nurse. She invariably knew more than the doctors when she worked in A and E. It's hardly surprising that she was frustrated, working in a village practice. A bit like putting a racehorse in a riding school, I suppose.'

Had she been frustrated? Alessandro abandoned the sandwich and ran a hand over the back of his neck, suddenly realising that it hadn't ever occurred to him that she was anything less than happy in her work. And he didn't like the fact that she'd confided in Jake. *Since when had Christy confided in Jake?* They were friends, that was true, but he didn't like the idea that his friend knew more about his wife than he did.

* * *

Checking that her mother was safely occupied in the kitchen, Katy slunk into the living room where her brother was orchestrating a battle between dinosaurs and toy soldiers.

'Ben, here's a really, really large glass of blackcurrant squash.'

Ben stared at it. 'I'm not thirsty.'

'Good,' Katy said sweetly, 'because I don't want you to drink it. I want you to spill it on the sofa.'

Ben's eyes widened. 'No way! You spill it on the sofa.'

'Don't be ridiculous.' Katy's tone was condescending. 'I'm eleven. I'm *way* past spilling drinks on the sofa. You'll have to do it.'

'But that will make the sofa wet and purple.'

'That's the general idea.'

'Why?'

'Because despite our efforts, our parents are still not sharing a bed,' Katy said with an impatient sigh. 'And they're never going to get back together if they don't share a bed. Everyone knows that adults should share a bed if they're married. It's how they mate.'

Ben picked up another dinosaur. 'What's mate?'

'You're far too young to understand,' Katy said disdainfully. 'You're just going to have to trust me.'

'I don't see how spilling blackcurrant squash will help,' Ben muttered, and Katy rolled her eyes.

'Because it will make the sofa sticky and wet you stupid, idiot baby.'

'I'm not a stupid, idiot baby!!'

'Then trust me and spill the squash!'

'Mum will be mad.'

Katy glared. 'Do you want to go back and live in smelly old London? Do you want Mum and Dad to live together again or not?'

Ben's face crumpled. 'Of course, I do, but—'

'Then spill it, Ben! Just spill it and stop asking questions!'

'But—'

'Ben, you spill things all the time.' Her tone was exasperated. 'You spilt your milk at breakfast. You dropped your pasta at supper. *Spill the blackcurrant before I strangle you!*'

'Mum says you're not allowed to put things round my neck. And if I spill blackcurrant, it will ruin the sofa.'

'That's the idea. Don't worry about that. It won't cost them anything because they can put in an insurance claim, but that will take weeks to come through,' Katy said airily, and Ben looked at her doubtfully.

Katy ground her teeth. 'Ben…'

'All right, I'll spill it.' Ben snatched the squash from her, sprinted across the living room, tripped over a toy he'd left there and spilt the entire contents of the glass over the sofa.

'Even better than I could have predicted,' Katy breathed, staring at the spreading, deep purple stain on the sofa with admiration and satisfaction. 'Well done, baby brother.'

Ben's lip wobbled as he stared at the mess. 'Mummy's going to be mad.'

'Very possibly,' Katy agreed, 'but she isn't going to be sleeping here tonight, and that's the only thing that matters. Don't worry, I'll protect you.'

'You shouldn't have had a drink in the living room.' Christy kept her voice level, reminding herself that it wasn't good to shout at one's children, especially when they were so clearly remorseful. Ben stood in front of her with his head down and his lip wobbling.

'Katy told me to do it!' He burst into sobs just as Alessandro walked in through the front door.

'What's going on here?'

Christy sighed, wondering whether everyone's family was as noisy and complicated as hers. 'I haven't had time to cook any dinner yet. Ben spilt blackcurrant all over the sofa. It's ruined.'

'Good thing,' Alessandro drawled, shrugging his broad shoulders out of his jacket and loosening his tie. 'It was ugly and uncomfortable and sleeping on it was having a detrimental effect on my spine. You've done me a favour, Ben.'

Katy appeared in the doorway, a yoghurt in one hand and a spoon in the other. 'That's decided, then. You'll just have to sleep in the bed with Mum.'

Alessandro turned to look at his daughter, a gleam of suspicion lighting his dark eyes. 'Are you behind this, Katherine?'

Katy took a few steps backwards. 'Don't look at me like that. It isn't good to intimidate your children. And you can't blame me for the fact that Ben spills everything. You *know* he spills everything.'

'Intimidate?' An ebony brow rose as Alessandro surveyed his daughter. 'Since when did I ever intimidate you?'

Ben's sobs grew noisier. 'It's all her fault. She made me do it and she—'

'Hush.' Christy pulled him into her arms and cuddled him close. 'I'm not mad with you, sweetie, honestly. Don't cry. Please, don't cry. It isn't important. It's only a sofa.'

'My house is turning into a war zone,' Alessandro muttered, dragging a hand through his dark hair and letting out a long breath. 'Seeing that you haven't cooked any dinner yet, let's go out.'

Katy's face brightened. 'Great idea. You'll need to get us a babysitter. I nominate Uncle Jake.'

Christy blinked. 'I think Daddy meant all of us.'

'Oh, no, we're much too tired to go out.' Katy gave an exaggerated yawn to prove her point. 'I've got holiday homework to finish and Ben needs his beauty sleep. Not that all the sleep in the world is going to make him half-decent to look at,' she added as an afterthought, and Ben sat up and poked his tongue out.

Alessandro gave a shrug and looked at Christy. 'So—you and I can go out.'

'But…' How could she say that she didn't really want to go out on a date that had been engineered by the children? If he'd asked her, that would have been different. 'Jake won't be free.'

'He's free—I saw him at lunchtime.' Alessandro was already on the phone, and Christy sighed.

'All right. I'll go and change.'

'Wear the black dress, Mummy,' Katy hissed, and Christy frowned.

'What black dress?'

'The little one that makes Daddy grab you from behind.'

Christy blushed and wondered at exactly what point her daughter had started noticing so much. 'That's a party dress, sweetheart.'

'So? You look pretty in it.'

Christy bit her lip. But did she want to look pretty? Yes, of course she did. But wearing a party dress to go out to dinner in the middle of the week would look desperate, and she had too much pride to show Alessandro just how desperate she was.

Crazy, she thought as she rummaged through her wardrobe. She was having an informal supper with her husband and she had absolutely no idea what to wear.

She wanted to look attractive, but not obvious. She wanted him to want her.

Wanted him to kiss her. Would that fix things? she wondered. If he kissed her and took her to bed, would they be able to heal their wounds?

In the end she settled for a slinky velvet skirt in a shade of heather and teamed it with a slinky black top that dipped temptingly at the front.

Jake walked through the door as she reached for her coat. He immediately strode over and kissed her. 'You look stunning and beautiful,' he breathed, his eyes lingering on the neckline of her top.

Glancing at Alessandro, Christy wondered why he was glaring. Presumably he was still annoyed at having their evening manipulated by the children.

Clearly he had no real wish to spend time with her. Unlike Jake, he hadn't even commented on what she was wearing.

Jake swept Ben into his arms and stooped to hug an excited Katy.

'Uncle Jake!'

'Did you bring me a present?' Ben wrapped his legs and arms around Jake like a monkey, and Christy gasped in horror and embarrassment at his question.

'You don't ask people that, Ben,' she admonished, but Jake just grinned.

'Why not? Honesty gets you a long way in life, I always think. If only women were as uncomplicated as children, life would run much more smoothly.' He whipped a bag out from behind his back. 'Sweets and a DVD and maybe a small toy because I haven't seen you for so long.'

'Finally, a grown-up who understands us.' Katy grinned, reaching into the bag to check out the DVD. 'I'm allowed to watch 12s now. This is a PG.'

'That's right. My psyche is sadly underdeveloped and I don't want to risk nightmares. I thought I'd be all right if you held my hand all the way through.' Jake winked at her, his smile placid. 'Lead me to your father's whisky cabinet, angel. I've had a long day.'

'We won't be late,' Christy began, but Katy frowned and pushed them towards the door.

'Don't come back before the end of the DVD or you'll spoil it.'

Christy sighed. 'Don't keep them up late, Jake.'

'Go and enjoy yourselves,' Jake said, delving into the bag he'd brought and producing a new dinosaur for Ben. 'We'll be fine.'

But would she? Christy wondered.

It had been so long since she'd spent an evening with Alessandro that she didn't quite know what they were going to talk about.

Alessandro took her to a noisy, Spanish tapas bar in the middle of town.

Disappointed that he hadn't chosen somewhere quiet and romantic, Christy slid into her chair and reached for a menu.

'We used to come here a lot when we first met—do you remember?'

'The service was quick and what with the hospital and the mountain rescue team, we never had enough time.' Alessandro turned to the hovering waiter and ordered in Spanish.

Christy closed the menu and tried not to mind that he hadn't asked what she wanted.

It was just the way Alessandro was, she thought with weary resignation. The dominant male. Always strong and controlling. At times, it was wonderful. In A and E, with a desperately sick patient, his astonishing leadership qualities saved lives. At home, just occasionally, it would be nice if he showed an interest in her views.

'So...' He lounged back in his chair and surveyed her across the table, his eyes glittering dark in the dim light of the restaurant, 'how are you enjoying being back in A and E?'

Given her thoughts of a few moments earlier, Christy was surprised he'd asked. 'I... Well, I really like it.'

'You're good.'

'And that surprises you?'

He gave a slow smile. 'No. What surprises me is that you seem to have forgotten nothing in the time that you've been away.'

Should she confess that it had surprised her, too? 'I suppose I worked there for so long that some of it is second nature.' She took a deep breath. 'Do you hate having me there?'

'It is impossible to hate someone who makes your working life easier,' he drawled, lifting his glass of wine. 'With so many people off sick and others inexperienced, it becomes difficult to deliver your best performance.'

'And that's so important, isn't it?'

'Of course.' He gave a shrug. 'The patient deserves no less.'

'That's true. But the patients are not your whole life. What about me?' Her voice was soft. 'Didn't our marriage deserve the same attention?'

His broad shoulders tensed. 'We're going to talk about this now? All right, let's talk about this now.' His eyes narrowed and his fingers tightened around the glass. 'We both had busy lives—'

'With no time for each other.' She folded her hands in her lap and looked him in the eye, de-termined to have her say. *Determined not to let him intimidate her.* 'Do you know how many times I scraped your dinner into the bin during the twelve years of our marriage, Alessandro?'

'My working hours are unpredictable, it's true, but—'

'How many times did we sit down together and talk during the week?'

'At the dinner table, rarely,' he admitted, 'but always we were in the same bed at night.'

The remark was so typical of him that she gave a wry smile. 'That's just sex, Alessandro.'

One ebony brow swooped upwards in silent mockery. *'Just* sex, *querida?'*

Her stomach rolled and fire licked through her veins. She wasn't going to think about sex now, she told herself frantically. She wasn't going to remember what it was like to be in bed with Alessandro. He was a spectacular lover.

'A relationship takes more than an encounter in the bedroom to keep it alive,' she said huskily, and he studied her in brooding silence.

'And that's why you left? You felt neglected? I didn't ask you about your day often enough?'

'I don't think you *ever* asked me about my day. You're a great father, a skilled and talented doctor, a fantastic climber...' She swallowed. 'But—'

'But I've been a lousy husband,' Alessandro drawled softly, and she shook her head quickly.

'Not lousy, no.' She gripped her glass. 'But you're so driven, so focused on what you do and…I suppose I feel as though you don't notice me any more.'

She wanted to ask about Katya. Wanted to know whether he'd had an affair during the weeks that they'd been apart. But something held her back. He wouldn't do that, she told herself. Alessandro wouldn't do that.

'How long have you hated being a practice nurse?'

She looked at him, surprised by the question. 'I don't hate it.' She hesitated. 'But I suppose part of me is always frustrated. I miss the pace and unpredictability of A and E. You know what it's like—sort of an addiction.'

He gave a wry smile. 'You get high on the adrenaline rush of not knowing what's coming through the door next?'

She returned the smile. 'Yes, in a way. In general practice it's all so much more predictable and routine. And a bit lonely. I was shut in a room all day, seeing an endless stream of patients. We have practice meetings, of course, and I speak to the GPs about various patients, but I miss the teamwork of A and E.'

Alessandro sat back in his chair as the waiter delivered plates of food to their table. 'So why have you stuck at it for so long?'

'Because it fits with school hours,' Christy said slowly, leaning forward to examine the various dishes he'd ordered. 'It's convenient for family life. But the children are older now…'

Should she tell him that she didn't think that she could go back? Should she tell him that, after experiencing the buzz of A and E again, she was starting to rethink her whole life?

'Why did you never tell me any of this before?'

She shrugged. 'What was the point? One of us had to be there for the children and that wasn't going to be you—you're not that sort of man. I knew that when I married you and that was fine. And, anyway, you had a great career. And I suppose I've never told you any of this before because…' She broke off, suddenly hesitant. 'Well, because you've never asked.'

'Perhaps because I assumed that if there was a problem you would tell me.' He frowned. 'I'm not great at guessing games and reading minds. That's more Jake's forte.'

'Jake. He's such a good person, isn't he?' Christy smiled to herself and missed the dangerous flash in Alessandro's eyes. 'I can't believe we've been friends for such a long time. And I can't understand why he hasn't settled down with some very lucky woman long before now.' She heard Alessandro's sharp intake of breath and glanced up.

'Perhaps he wants someone who is unavailable,' he snapped. His tone was icy cold and she looked at him, surprised by the comment.

'Oh, no! Jake isn't like that. He'd never go after a married woman.'

'But if she wasn't married any more, she'd be fair game,' Alessandro said tightly. 'Isn't that right?'

'Well, I suppose so. Maybe.' Christy stared at him, wondering why he suddenly seemed so tense and moody. Had she said something? 'Anyway, why are we talking about Jake?'

There was a long, pulsing silence while Alessandro studied her and drummed his fingers on the table. 'He just seemed to come up in conversation,' he said silkily, and she gave a puzzled smile.

'Well, we've all known each other and been friends for the same length of time, so I suppose that's natural.' She helped herself to a spoonful of another dish and tried not to mind that Alessandro suddenly seemed tense and uncommunicative.

He didn't enjoy her company any more, she thought miserably as she chewed her way through a mouthful of food that she didn't even want. And he still hadn't said anything about what she was wearing or made a single move in her direction.

It was so unlike him. In the past, whenever they'd had a problem, he'd just grabbed her and that had been that. Now he didn't seem to want to touch her.

Was it because he didn't find her attractive any more?

Or was it because he was seeing someone else?

Back in the barn, the DVD had just finished and Ben was changing into his pyjamas in front of the fire.

'Uncle Jake, what's mating?'

Jake choked on his whisky. 'Well, I...' He cleared his throat and vowed never to babysit again. 'Ben, you've had seven years to ask that question. Why do you have to ask it now, while Mummy is out?'

'Because Katy said it earlier,' Ben said solemnly, wriggling his arms and head into his pyjama top. 'She said that we have to get Mummy and Daddy back into the same bedroom so that they can mate. It's why I broke the bed and spilled my drink.'

Jake gave up on the whisky. 'You did *what*?'

'I broke the bed,' Ben said patiently, 'by bouncing hard. Katy did it, too. So Mummy couldn't sleep there any more. But it didn't work.'

Jake put his glass down on the nearest table. 'It didn't?'

Ben shook his head. 'Daddy went and slept on the sofa, so I spilt my blackcurrant on it.'

Jake's gaze slid to the sofa on the far side of the room, now covered in towels. 'So you did.'

'Now Daddy *has* to sleep with Mummy in the bed,' Ben said proudly, and Jake looked at him thoughtfully before shifting his gaze to Katy.

'It appears that you've been rather busy, young lady.'

'You can't tell me off. You're my godfather. You're only responsible for my religious education.'

He lifted a brow. 'No more presents, then.'

She grinned. 'Presents are acceptable.'

'I just bet they are.' Jake studied her face and thought how much she resembled her father. 'Have you been interfering?'

'Maybe. Just a little.' Her expression was wary, as if she was unsure of his response. 'Never underestimate a child.'

'I don't,' Jake said dryly, rising to his feet and reaching for his glass. He had a strong feeling he was going to need a large refill. 'Let's get your brother to bed and then you and I need to have a talk, Katherine Isabel Luisa Garcia. You have some *serious* explaining to do.'

CHAPTER FIVE

'You look knackered.' Nicky juggled an armful of dressings and frowned as Christy walked onto the unit. 'Heavy night?' She gave a saucy wink and Christy gave a wan smile.

What would Nicky say, she wondered, if she confessed that she'd spent the night lying next to Alessandro and he hadn't laid a finger on her? Not only that, but he'd clearly had no trouble sleeping, whereas she'd lain there, tense and breathless, waiting for him to touch her. His steady, rhythmic breathing had done nothing for her ego or her hopes for the survival of their marriage.

Oh, damn, damn, damn.

He obviously didn't even find her attractive any more. It was the only possible explanation for not touching her.

And just to bolster her insecurities still further,

Katya chose that moment to stroll up to them. 'Hi, there.' Her voice was smoky and seductive and her blonde hair fell down her back in a perfect, smooth sheet. She wore a pale pink roll-neck jumper and a tight navy skirt that ended just above the knee, and could have walked straight out of the pages of a glossy magazine. 'Have either of you seen Alessandro? He promised to spend some time talking me through some interesting X-rays.'

Christy gritted her teeth and swallowed hard. She wasn't going to be jealous, she told herself. She wasn't going to be paranoid or childish. So, the girl was beautiful. That didn't mean anything…

'Alessandro is with a head injury patient in Resus,' Nicky said in a cool tone, 'and I need you to tie your hair back in this department, please. It's unhygienic worn loose.'

Katya frowned slightly and then shrugged. 'No problem. I have some grips in my bag.'

'Good.' Nicky gave a brisk nod, very much the sister-in-charge. 'I'd appreciate it if you'd use them.'

Katya strolled off and Nicky stared after her,

still clutching the dressing packs to her chest. 'I don't like that girl. Where does she think she is? On a catwalk?'

'She looks great.' Christy said with a forced smile, and Nicky grinned.

'Oh, yeah—and how great is she going to look when a drunk has vomited down her pink cashmere? Are you OK? You look pale.'

'Just a bit tired.'

'Look…' Nicky put a hand on her arm, her gaze sympathetic, 'I know things are rough for you and Alessandro at the moment, but I know you'll work it out. The two of you were meant to be together.'

Were they?

She was starting to wonder.

'There you are!' Sean strode down the corridor towards them, interrupting them in mid-conversation. 'Christy, the mountain rescue team have had a call about a man who has fallen some distance. Might have chest and head injuries. The details are a bit hazy but we're trying to send an advance party of five out, with the rest of the team following.'

Christy stared at him blankly. 'And?' What did it have to do with her? She hadn't been out with the MRT for several years.

'We're a bit thin on the ground in the team at the moment,' Sean said wearily. 'Everyone is either in bed with this flu bug or they're snowed in or all sorts of other feeble excuses. Alessandro is going and I wondered if you'd join him in the advance party.'

'Me?' Christy's voice was an astonished squeak and Sean gave her a keen look.

'Why not you? You're fit and you know these mountains. You were the best climber we had at one time.'

Christy licked her lips. 'Yes, but I had the kids and—'

'I wasn't aware that childbirth affected your mountaineering abilities,' Sean drawled, glancing round as Alessandro approached. 'Garcia, just the man. I'm trying to persuade your wife to join you on this callout while I scrabble around and try and get some other people together.'

Alessandro's brows met in a frown. 'Christy?'

'Why does everyone think it's such a strange idea?' Sean wondered aloud, and Alessandro's mouth tightened.

'Because the weather is foul and I don't want her risking—'

'I'll go,' Christy said immediately, turning to Nicky. 'If that's all right with you?'

Alessandro didn't think she could do it, and she was determined to prove him wrong, just as she had by working in A and E. What was the matter with the man?

'I'm used to it.' Nicky gave a resigned smile. 'I'll just run the department on fresh air as usual.'

'My walking boots are in the car but all my other gear is at home.'

'You can use Ally's gear,' Sean was already walking towards the door. 'You're about the same size. My dear wife never gets round to removing it from my boot. Come on.'

As they walked towards the car Christy's anger at Alessandro mingled with excitement. Ahead of them the fells loomed, covered in snow and ice and potentially lethal. Who had gone walking in this weather? she wondered. How had they got themselves into trouble?

'You stick right by me,' Alessandro growled as they slid into his car, and she turned and glared at him.

'Why? In case I fall down a hole? For crying out loud, Alessandro, when I was twenty I could outclimb you any day!'

It wasn't strictly true and she saw by the lift of his eyebrow that he was aware of that fact, but he didn't contradict her.

'You're not twenty any more.'

'No, I'm thirty-two. Ancient.' She stared at him in disbelief. 'Is this what this is all about? You think I'm suddenly too old to do these things?'

'It has nothing to do with age.' Alessandro crunched the gears viciously. 'You're the mother of my children.'

'And what? That means I should stay at home and knit?' Her voice rose and she took a deep breath and forced herself to calm down. 'Giving birth to children doesn't come with a person- ality transplant. Believe it or not, I'm still the same person I was twelve years ago when you first met me!'

'You can't just swan up a mountain when you haven't been near one for years.'

'That's rubbish! I may not have been on the team, but I've done plenty of climbing and walking and I'm every bit as fit as you are!'

The atmosphere in the car was simmering with mounting tension and she looked away, so angry that she wanted to hit something. Or someone.

'Fine.' His voice was tight as he concentrated on keeping the car on the road in the lethal conditions. 'Just no heroics.'

'Heroics?' She turned and glared at him as she tugged a hat onto her head. 'Since when have I suffered from a hero complex?'

'You always took risks when you were climbing.'

'That's *not* true.'

'As you said yourself, you haven't been with the team for a long time.' Alessandro changed gear with a vicious thrust of his hand. 'What you've forgotten could prove dangerous. I just don't want your ego to get in the way. If you don't know something, say so.'

'What I know is that I'm not the one with the ego around here,' she spat angrily, jamming her feet into her boots and yanking so hard at the laces that she almost snapped them. 'There's only room in this car for one ego and yours is taking up all the space!'

He had no confidence in her whatsoever, she thought, her temper building to dangerous levels. 'I hadn't been in A and E for years either,' she pointed out angrily, 'but so far I haven't killed anyone! This used to be my life, Alessandro! This was what I did, but somewhere along the way I've lost it all. I've lost A and E, I've lost Mountain Rescue and now I've lost—' She had been about to say 'you' but she stopped herself just in time. Instead, she clamped her teeth down on her bottom lip and blinked back the hot sting of tears.

His opinion of her was obviously at rock bottom, she thought miserably as she turned her head and stared out of the window while she struggled for control.

He slowed down to take an icy corner. 'You make it sound as though your entire married life has been one big sacrifice.'

'No.' Confident that she was back in control again, she turned her head and studied his hard, handsome profile. *She loved him so much.* Despite everything, she completely adored him and always would. 'That isn't how it is. The children are everything. But there are parts of me that I put to one side while they were small and you can't blame me for wanting them back now.'

Alessandro was silent, his strong hands gripping the steering-wheel. 'I had no idea that you missed it so badly.' His voice was a low growl and she swallowed hard, her anger dissolving to nothing, suddenly desperate to make him understand.

'Wouldn't you miss it? If you were the one who had to give it all up, wouldn't you miss it?'

'That's different.'

'How is it different, Alessandro? Because you're a man and I'm a woman?' Her temper boiled up again and she resisted the temptation to thump him hard. 'Well, I've got news for you, my Neanderthal, chauvinistic male, it isn't different at all! Which marriage rule book says that it's the woman who has to make all the changes in her life?'

He inhaled sharply. 'You knew when you married me that I wasn't the sort of man who could stay at home and change nappies, but if you'd wanted a nanny you could have said so.'

'I didn't want a nanny! I wanted to be the one to raise our children.' She was shouting now, shouting as she zipped up her jacket and reached for her gloves. 'But I'm allowed to be honest about missing some bits of my old life. And I'm also allowed to see if I want some of those bits back now that the children are older. Is that really asking too much?'

Alessandro flicked the indicator and pulled into the car park at the mountain rescue base. Then he switched off the engine and sat staring into the freezing cold December day, his handsome face blank of expression. 'No,' he said finally. 'It isn't asking too much.'

'When we first met, we were doing the same things,' she said, suddenly desperate to say the things that had been building inside her for months. 'We were on the same path. But somehow that's all changed. You've gone on ahead and I've been left behind.'

He turned towards her. 'Is that how you see it?'

'No,' she said quietly. 'It's just how it is.'

She wanted to ask where that left their relationship but he seemed so distant and icily remote that she didn't know what to say and was relieved to see Jake and two other members of the MRT striding across the car park towards them.

'Oh, great—there's Jake.' Grateful for a reason to escape from the chill inside the car, she opened the door and slid out.

Alessandro sat for a moment, simmering with mounting tension, the expression in his dark eyes approaching dangerous as he watched her greet Jake with a warm hug.

Had she always been so demonstrative with Jake?

Why had he never noticed how physical they were before now?

He knew that Jake found Christy attractive but never before this moment had he had reason to ask questions about where Christy's affections lay because he'd always known that she adored *him*. He'd been utterly secure in their love.

From the first day they'd met, he'd taken her adoration and devotion for granted. They had been so crazy about each other, *so hot for each other*, that it had never entered his head that she would ever look at another man.

But something had obviously changed over the years and now it seemed that Jake knew things about Christy that he didn't. Private, intimate things. Like the fact that she'd never really been happy as a practice nurse. And the fact that she missed bits of her old life.

Alessandro stared out of the window and his mouth tightened.

He should have known those things about his wife.

Why hadn't she told him? Why had Jake been easier to talk to? Experiencing self-doubt for one of the few times in his adult life, Alessandro cursed softly and reached into the back seat for the rest of his gear.

He'd get this rescue out of the way and then he was going to sort this out.

He loved her. He loved her desperately and keeping his distance from her was turning him into a crazy man. But if she was in love with Jake then he'd give her the freedom she wanted. Wasn't that what you were supposed to do with someone you loved? Set them free?

Christy lifted the pack onto her back, careful not to look at Alessandro.

He didn't think that she could do this, but she was going to prove him wrong. Prove that she was more that just the mother of his children.

'According to the call we had, he was one of four walkers taking a path just below the summit,' Alessandro said as he assembled the advance party. 'They called the police on a mobile and one of them had a global positioning instrument so we've got a good idea where they are.'

'Weather's looking unfriendly,' Jake observed as he lifted his pack onto his back and settled it comfortably. 'Might need to carry him off the hill if the helicopter can't fly in this.'

Alessandro nodded. 'That's a distinct possibility. One of his group reported that he had breathing difficulties so we're carrying an oxygen cylinder just in case. All right, let's go.'

He strode out in front and Christy walked behind him, hoping that she wasn't going to fall down gasping for breath because that would be too humiliating for words. She was fit, she reminded herself. And she knew these mountains as well as she knew her own back garden. The fact that she hadn't been part of a proper rescue for a few years really didn't signify. Once it had been a huge part of her life. The regular training sessions, callouts, social events—she'd done it all and she'd loved every minute of it. And all that knowledge was still there, she reminded herself.

All the same, she was quite relieved to be sandwiched between Alessandro and Jake. Having someone in front and behind made it easier to resist the temptation to slow the pace.

They walked steadily for two hours in decreasing visibility and deteriorating weather conditions and then heard shouts from up ahead.

'Bingo,' Jake murmured, as they pushed on through the swirling snow and mist and finally saw torches and bright jackets on the path ahead.

By now Christy's cheeks were stinging with

cold and her eyelashes were wet and clumped together. But she loved being outdoors in the mountains. The wind had picked up, the weather was wild and unforgiving and it all seemed as far from the rain-washed streets of London as it was possible to be.

The injured man was sitting propped against a rock, covered in several coats. There was blood on his forehead and he had a hand on his chest, his face crumpled in pain. Hope lit his eyes as he saw them trudge towards him through the mist and snow.

Crouching next to him, offering moral support, was one of his fellow walkers, and he stood up as they arrived, his relief plainly visible on his tired features. 'Boy, am I glad to see you! My first aid isn't up to the challenge, I'm afraid. He fell about twenty feet,' he told them, 'and since then he's had real trouble with his breathing. It's really noisy. He was really struggling so I sat him up—I hope I did the right thing. I know you're not supposed to move an injured person, but—'

'You've done well,' Christy assured him quickly, heaving her rucksack off her back.

Alessandro was already reaching for the oxygen, his movements as decisive as ever.

That was one of the things she loved and admired about him, Christy thought to herself. Some doctors were fine as long as they were in a hospital, surrounded by high-tech equipment and a phone to give them access to doctors from different specialities. Alessandro was equally cool and self-assured when he was halfway up a mountain in a blizzard with a potentially seriously injured patient.

He was a man who thrived on challenge and she'd always found his inner strength and bold self-confidence incredibly seductive. There was no situation that Alessandro wouldn't be able to handle.

Ignoring her aching shoulders, she dropped to her knees beside him, trying to ignore the angry howl of the icy wind that threatened to obliterate her vision.

'His name is Simon Duke,' the friend volunteered, 'and he's fifty-two.'

'Did you see what happened?' She knew that an account of the accident might give clues as to the injuries they were potentially dealing with.

'We've been out since early this morning. We'd just started our descent when Simon slipped.' He pulled a face. 'I've been climbing and walking in the mountains for most of my life. I never thought I'd be calling on the services of the mountain rescue team. To say that I'm finding this highly embarrassing would be a major understatement.'

'It happens to the best of us,' Jake said cheerfully, squinting through the blizzard as he heaved the pack off his back and removed the oxygen cylinder he'd been carrying. The snow was now blowing horizontally and their packs had started to freeze. 'I must say, you chose fabulous weather for your walk.'

'Ignore him, he's deranged,' Christy said dryly, then glanced towards Alessandro for guidance. 'If he fell twenty feet then he should probably be wearing a collar?'

'Definitely. But we also need to get him into a shelter while I check him over.' Alessandro reached into his rucksack and pulled out the necessary equipment. 'Jake, get that oxygen going and let's get him into a bivvy tent so that I can examine him properly. We're going to have to carry him off because there's no way they can fly a helicopter in this.'

Simon gasped and closed his eyes briefly. 'So sorry to be such a nuisance,' he panted. 'Can't believe I need oxygen.'

'I'm glad you do,' Jake drawled as he removed his gloves so that he could adjust the flow rate. 'If I'd lugged this canister all the way up this hill for nothing, I would have been steaming mad.' He handed the mask to Christy and she fixed the mask over the man's mouth and nose.

'There.' She spoke gently. 'That should help. We're just going to get you some shelter before you get too cold.'

Jake moved across to help Alessandro with the shelter. 'Has anyone placed a bet on a white Christmas?'

'We always have a white Christmas up here.' Noticing how pale Simon looked, Christy checked his pulse while her team members erected a tent. She glanced up at the patient's walking companion. 'So was this a pre-Christmas holiday?'

'Supposed to be.' He gave a rueful smile. 'We were making the most of a few days' peace and quiet before we go down to London for Christmas.'

'And he slipped?'

'Just seemed to lose his footing. I suppose there must have been a patch of ice on the rock,' the man shrugged. 'One minute he was walking along happily, in front of me, the next he was slithering downwards. Gave me a bad moment, I can tell you. I think he managed to grab hold of a rock or something, otherwise goodness knows how far he would have fallen.'

The injured man tried to say something and Christy put a hand on his shoulder and shook her head. 'Don't talk, Simon,' she said quickly. 'We'll soon have you inside the bivvy tent and then the doctor can look at you.'

His companion looked at her in surprise. 'He's a doctor?'

'You've got half the A and E department up here,' Jake said cheerfully, walking back across to them, 'and just to cap it, if you want a baby delivered then I'm your man.'

Christy giggled and then caught something

black in Alessandro's gaze and her laughter faded. What was the matter with him? Normally he found Jake as amusing as she did.

Soon Simon was safely inside the protective covering of the tent and Christy saw more lights flashing through the snow. 'Looks like the rest of the team are arriving.'

'More? Obviously we've bothered a great number of people.'

'It takes a lot of people to stretcher someone off a mountain,' Christy explained. She stuck her head inside the bivvy tent and Alessandro looked up from his examination.

'He has broken ribs and a broken ankle. He's not showing any signs of a pneumothorax,' he said swiftly, 'so I'm going to splint the ankle and give him some analgesia and get him off this hill before he gets hypothermia.'

Christy helped him stabilise the injured walker and get him into a fleece-lined casualty bag.

The rest of the team joined them and Christy helped them put together the two halves of a stretcher that would be used to carry the casualty down off the mountain. It was a task that they'd practised over and over again during training evenings, assembling the stretcher as fast as possible. Once, she recalled, they'd even done it in the dark to try and mimic the conditions they might face on the mountain. Now, with Alessandro's gaze resting on her all too frequently, she was glad of that training. Glad that she knew exactly what to do and wasn't letting herself down.

Only when they were ready did they remove the shelter that was protecting their casualty.

By now, a team of twenty-five had assembled and one of the other MRT members stood at the head of the stretcher and acted as an anchor to prevent the stretcher moving downhill while it was being prepared for evacuation.

Alessandro made another check on his patient and then tied a rope to the stretcher with a bowline knot.

'We're going to have to do this very carefully,' he instructed, 'because he's already suffering from chest injuries.'

'How do I know you're not going to drop me?' Simon said weakly, and Christy smiled.

'Because you've got ten bulky guys holding onto the stretcher and a rope as back-up. And if we drop you, we're fired.'

The man managed a smile. 'You're all volunteers.'

'You think we do this for nothing?' Jake's blue eyes gleamed with wicked humour as he tightened the straps. 'That would make me certifiably insane, don't you think?'

Christy heaved her pack onto her back. 'Well, now that you mention it…'

How had she survived without this? she wondered. The comradeship and the banter. The physical challenge of extracting someone from a perilous situation.

Eventually everyone was satisfied, the safety checks had been made and the team started their descent, picking their way over boulders made treacherous by ice and snow. Whenever possible, they sledged the stretcher down the mountain and finally the mist and snow cleared and the road came into sight.

As Christy slithered and slipped, she noticed Alessandro constantly glancing in her direction.

Checking up on her?

The MRT vehicle that doubled as an ambulance was waiting.

'You're only a ten-minute drive from the hospital,' Christy told Simon as they carried him the final few metres. 'They'll soon have you comfortable.'

He shook his head. 'My wife is going to kill me. She's always telling me I'm too old to be walking in the hills.'

'Ignore her,' Jake advised cheerfully as he yanked open the back of the vehicle and prepared to lift the stretcher inside. 'What do women know about anything?' He winked at Christy and she gave a wan smile.

Thanks to Alessandro, she was starting to feel as though she knew nothing.

Leaving the rest of the work to their colleagues, Jake pulled her gently to one side and gave her a searching look. 'You all right, babe?'

'Of course.' Behind her, they were loading the injured man into the ambulance. 'Why wouldn't I be?'

'Hey.' Jake frowned. 'This is me you're talking

to. Not some stranger. I can tell you're not all right. I don't suppose the look on your face has anything to do with the broken bed and the ruined sofa?'

Her eyes widened. 'You know about that?'

'I talk to my goddaughter.' For once, Jake's expression was serious. 'Obviously things aren't going that well between the two of you. I assumed that once you were under the same roof, you'd be able to sort your problems out.'

'I thought so, too.' Her voice was husky and suddenly she had a wild impulse to throw herself against Jake's broad shoulders and cry her eyes out. *She badly needed a hug.* 'But I was wrong.' She glanced across to where Alessandro was standing, his glossy dark hair touched by the snow, his manner autocratic and confident as he talked to one of his fellow team members. 'He doesn't want me any more, Jake. He doesn't love me.'

Her voice broke on the words and Jake swore under his breath and pulled her into his arms. 'Don't cry,' he said softly, his hands gently smoothing her back. 'You're wrong, Christy. He does love you.'

She pulled away from him, embarrassed at her sudden loss of control. Ashamed to have revealed something so private, even to their oldest and dearest friend. 'No.' She shook her head. 'I hoped he did, but I was just deluding myself.'

'What makes you say that?'

'When I went down to London, he didn't come after me.'

'You wanted him to?'

'Of course I did, you stupid oaf! What sort of a question is that?' She gave him a watery smile. 'I thought you were supposed to understand women?'

'Me?' Jake pretended to look baffled. 'Oh, that's just an act I put on to help me pull. It never fails. What else makes you think he doesn't love you?'

She bit her lip. 'We haven't…been close since I came home and that's not like him. Normally he's very…' She blushed slightly, embarrassed that she was revealing so much. 'Very physical.'

Jake's gaze was steady on her face. 'Perhaps he's giving you space.'

She shook her head. 'Alessandro is much too selfish for that,' she muttered. 'If he wants something, he goes after it and he gets it. You know what he's like.'

'I think he's just taken his eye off the ball.' Jake stretched out a hand to remove some snow from her hair. 'It's good to have you back on the team.'

'Alessandro doesn't think so,' she said, unable to keep the hurt out of her voice. 'He thinks that all I'm capable of is picking up after the children. He doesn't see me as a woman any more.'

'Doesn't he?' For a moment, Jakc's expression was thoughtful. Then he smiled. 'Hang in there, babe. Everything is going to be fine.'

She rolled her eyes, touched by his comment but lacking his optimism. 'It's sweet of you to say so, but how can everything possibly be fine, you great dope?'

He treated her to the smile that had women lusting after him in droves. 'Because this is Christmas, my angel. Peace on earth and goodwill to all men. The time for miracles and forgiveness. Why don't you just be patient and see what special gift Santa brings you this year?'

'I don't think Santa does marriage rescue, does

he?' She still didn't see how any of it could be fine, but she appreciated his efforts to make her feel better, so she smiled. 'Thank you,' she said softly, touching his arm with her hand, 'for being a good friend.'

He stared down at her thoughtfully. 'You're a beautiful, sexy woman, Christy,' he said quietly. 'If I'd seen you first, you would have been mine. But Alessandro fell in love with you on sight and there was no contest. You never even noticed me.'

She stood in stunned silence, her eyes wide. She'd never realised that he felt that way. She didn't know what to say. How was she supposed to respond? 'Jake, I—'

'Fight for him, Christianna,' Jake said quietly, a lopsided smile on his face. 'I stepped aside because I could see the strength of what you shared. I've always seen it. Always envied it. Why do you think I haven't married before now? Because I've seen what love can be and I won't settle for anything less. Fight for it, babe.'

She stared up at him. 'But if I'm right that Alessandro doesn't love me any more then…'

Jake shrugged. 'Then all you'll be left with is damaged pride, and what's pride when the love of your life is at stake? Live up to the promise of your furious, angry hair, sweetheart, and fight.'

She stood in silence with the snow falling all around her and the temperature dropping to well below freezing. There was a shriek of a siren as the ambulance took off towards the hospital and the slamming of car doors as the various members of the mountain rescue team sorted out their equipment.

He was right, of course, she thought, feeling the snow flutter past her cheeks. Instead of playing these silly games, she should be fighting for her man. Trying to win him back. She'd never been one to give up when things got tough. That wasn't how she was.

Alessandro was the only man she'd ever loved. *The only man she ever could love.*

A smile spread across her face and, on impulse, she stood on tiptoe and kissed Jake on the cheek.

'Thank you,' she whispered. 'For being the very best friend to both of us.'

Then she turned and walked back to the car

and didn't notice Alessandro staring after her, the expression in his dark eyes bordering on the dangerous.

CHAPTER SIX

'MUM, can we go to the forest to choose our tree tomorrow?'

Christy looked up from injecting brandy into the Christmas cake. 'I— Yes, why not? We usually get it the week before Christmas.'

'And is Dad coming, too?'

Christy inhaled sharply. *How was she supposed to know?* Alessandro had hardly spoken to her since they'd returned from the mountain rescue the day before. At work he'd been cold and distant and he'd arrived home late and come to bed long after her.

'Well…'

'Of course I'm coming.' Alessandro strolled into the room, still bare-chested after his shower, his jaw dark with stubble. 'Family ritual— choosing the biggest tree in the forest.'

Christy felt her insides drop with longing. She wanted to slide her hands over his bronzed, muscular body—wanted to feel his hands on her. Suddenly she had a disturbingly vivid mental picture of his hard body coming down on hers and—

'Christy?'

She snapped out of her erotic daydream and realised that he was watching her with a slumberous expression on his handsome face. *Did he know?* she wondered. *Did he know that she'd been imagining the two of them together?*

'Sorry.' The croak in her voice betrayed her. 'Did you say something?'

'I said that we are both going to the Snow Ball tomorrow night,' he said in that slightly accented drawl that always sent her pulse racing. 'Your mother has offered to babysit.'

'Oh…' Her heart fluttered. She couldn't remember the last time they'd gone out together, let alone to the Snow Ball. It was held every Christmas for all the hospital staff but usually Alessandro was working.

Her heart lifted at the prospect of a proper evening out.

It would be her chance to dress up.

To remind him that the mother of his children was also a living, breathing sexual woman.

If she was going to follow Jake's advice and fight, then what better place to start than at a party?

Ben frowned. 'But if you go out then it means you can't read my story.'

'I'll read your story.' Katy elbowed her brother hard and beamed at both of them. 'Sounds great! A lovely, family day. Christmas tree followed by Snow Ball. Can't wait.'

Alessandro's dark gaze slid towards his daughter. 'You don't mind having a babysitter again?'

'Mind? Why would we mind?'

Ben opened his mouth but closed it again in response to his sister's quelling look.

Why was he suggesting the party? Christy wondered. Was Alessandro suddenly keen to mend fences, too?

But then she remembered that, apart from that one passionate kiss at the hospital, he hadn't once laid a finger on her. It was so unlike him that the only possible explanation was that he just didn't find her attractive any more.

But Jake was right and she wasn't going to give up without a fight.

She bit her lip and mentally ran through the contents of her wardrobe.

The situation merited something new. Something sexy and feminine. There was a little boutique not far from the hospital. If she spoke to Nicky and skipped food, she should just about have time at lunchtime.

Alessandro poured himself a coffee and ran a hand over his rough jaw. 'I need to go and shave,' he said gruffly, 'I'll see you at work.'

The heavy snow had played havoc with the roads and pavements and A and E was crowded with people who had slipped on the ice.

'Show me another Colles' fracture and I'm resigning,' Nicky groaned as she carried a pile of X-rays towards fracture clinic. 'I wish people would just stay at home and watch television. I can't remember when I last ate and I am *starving*.'

At that moment the ambulance hotline rang and Nicky scooped up the phone, tucking the X-rays under her arm as she listened and asked questions.

'Child swallowed mother's iron tablets,' she called out as she replaced the phone, 'ETA five minutes. Will you and Alessandro take this one because I must get round to fracture clinic.'

Christy nodded and Alessandro came striding down the corridor in a dark suit that emphasised the width of his shoulders.

'He's been upstairs with the powers that be, arguing for more staff,' Nicky muttered as he strode towards them, 'and judging from the black look on his face, he didn't win. Can't imagine why. He always intimidates me when he's in one of his cold moods.'

'Two sides to a coin,' Christy muttered, and Nicky frowned.

'Sorry?'

Christy shook her head. 'Nothing.' But she knew that underneath his sometimes remote, chilly exterior was a boiling, red-hot passion capable of erupting with volcanic force.

'Despite having lived in this country for the past twelve years, sometimes I still think there is a language barrier,' Alessandro growled, and then switched into a flow of rapid Spanish that was incomprehensible to all except Christy.

Nicky blinked and turned to Christy. 'All right, you're married to the guy—translation, please.'

Christy smiled. She knew enough Spanish to have picked up the gist of his tirade and most of it wasn't polite. 'He's basically saying that they weren't that sympathetic but he told them that we need more staff or the unit will have to close,' she said smoothly, choosing to leave out the blunter aspects of Alessandro's invective.

Alessandro lifted an eyebrow in mockery. 'Selective translation, *querida*?'

'My Spanish isn't good enough,' Christy lied, but her eyes twinkled. 'There were several words that I didn't recognise.'

Alessandro stared at her for a long moment and her heart rate started to increase.

Nicky cleared her throat. 'I hate to interrupt this little multi-cultural interlude but if you'd stop gibbering in a foreign language for a moment, I might be able to hand over the details of this child and get to X-Ray before some sad patient complains about the level of service in this place. I don't want to be tomorrow's headlines in the tabloids, if it's all the same to you. Call me fussy, but "Patients Abandoned by Killer Nurse" wouldn't make my mum's day.'

Alessandro dragged his gaze away from Christy's. 'What child?'

'They're bringing in a child who has ingested iron,' Christy said, and Alessandro's eyes narrowed.

'How much?'

'Don't know that,' Nicky muttered, checking her notes, 'just that he's six years old and he's swallowed his mother's tablets. Big panic. On their way in as we speak. Off you go, guys. Save lives. But do it in English or no one will have a clue what you're talking about.'

And with that she stalked down the corridor, still juggling the X-rays and muttering about her grumbling stomach as the sound of an ambulance siren grew louder.

'I'll bleep the paediatricians and an anaesthetist,' Christy said, and Alessandro gave a nod.

'I'll meet the ambulance and see you in Paediatric Resus.'

The child was crying miserably and Christy

felt her heart twist. He reminded her so much of Ben. Instinctively she stepped towards the little boy but Alessandro was there before her.

'There, now,' he said softly, squatting down so that he was at the same level as the boy. 'Today is my lucky day because you have come to visit me in my special wizard's laboratory.'

The little boy's lip continued to wobble but he stared at Alessandro with wide eyes. 'Wizard?'

'Of course.' He waved a hand around the room. 'This is where I do all my experiments.' He reached into the pocket of his trousers, removed a coin and promptly made it disappear. The boy gasped in delight when it was 'retrieved' from his ear.

Christy grinned. That was Ben's favourite trick, too.

'Hide something else,' the little boy said in a small voice, and the mother gave a wobbly smile.

'Luke's always hiding things. You should see what I find in his pockets.' She bit her lip and looked at Christy, her expression full of guilt. 'I can't believe this has happened. I didn't even know those tablets were dangerous,' she whispered as she moved closer to the trolley. 'You can buy iron over the counter so I didn't really think it was too bad, but I had a friend with me and she said that iron can be lethal.' She covered her hand with her mouth and Alessandro gave Christy a sharp frown.

Interpreting his look, Christy took the mother to one side. Alessandro was successfully calming the child down—he didn't need the mother upsetting him again. 'The important thing right now is to find out how much he has taken and treat him,' she said gently. 'Did you bring the bottle?'

'Oh, yes…' The woman stuck her hand into her coat pocket and pulled out a bottle. 'It's supposed to have a childproof cap.'

'Some children are born dexterous and inquisitive,' Christy said dryly, thinking of Ben's antics.

The mother reached for a tissue and blew her nose. 'I can't believe he took them,' she whispered, her face blotched with tears. 'Or that I was stupid enough to leave them on the kitchen table. He said they looked like sweets. I only turned my back for a moment—'

'All drugs, even vitamins, should be kept well

out of reach of children, but the important thing now is to assess how many he's taken,' Christy said. 'Let's just concentrate on sorting him out. Try not to be upset because your distress will make him worse.'

Alessandro took the bottle and examined it. 'Do you know how many were in here?'

The mother shook her head. 'It was a full bottle last week and I haven't missed a dose, so quite a few.'

'And has he been sick?'

Again the mother shook her head and Christy held out her hand. 'I'll count the tablets,' she suggested, 'and that will give us an idea how many he's swallowed.'

At that moment, Billy hurried into the room to help, closely followed by the paediatric registrar.

'The important thing is the amount of elemental iron that has been ingested,' Alessandro told Billy in response to his question about iron poisoning.

Christy counted the tablets. 'Eight missing.' It was a lot, but Alessandro's expression didn't change.

'All right,' he said calmly, removing his jacket.

'We need to check his serum iron, glucose, do a full blood count. And let's get a plain, abdominal X-ray.'

Billy looked at him. 'X-ray?'

'Iron is radio-opaque,' Christy said quickly, 'the iron will show up on X-ray.' But as she studied the child, a thought flickered to life in the back of her mind. 'Luke, what did the tablets taste like?'

Alessandro frowned at her, clearly anxious to progress, but she lifted a hand and waited for Luke to answer.

'Sweets.' But he didn't quite meet her eyes and an instinct made her step closer to the trolley.

'Luke.' She kept her voice gentle. 'Did you swallow the sweets or did you hide them?' She saw something in his eyes and her conviction grew. 'No one is going to be angry with you, sweetheart,' she said softly. 'But we need to know the truth. Are they in your pockets?'

There was a long silence and then Luke nodded, his eyes huge. 'I was keeping them for later.'

Ignoring the gasp that came from his mother, Christy held out her hand to the little boy. 'Show me.'

After a moment's hesitation, Luke dug a hand into his pocket and pulled out a handful of tablets, now covered in fluff and bits of sweet paper. He dropped them into Christy's palm and she counted them quickly.

'Eight,' she said in a calm voice. 'They're all here, Alessandro. If Mrs Kennet hasn't missed a single tablet, that makes this a full bottle.'

The paediatrician breathed a sigh of relief and backed out of the room and the mother started to scold Luke, but Christy interrupted her quickly.

'Good boy, Luke,' she said firmly. 'Good boy for telling the truth.'

'But why didn't he tell us sooner?' Mrs Kennet asked, a baffled expression on her face, and Luke dipped his head.

'You were yelling and screaming and then the ambulance came and that was really cool with the light and the bell thing…'

Christy glanced at Alessandro and saw the gleam of amusement in his eyes. And relief. He was thinking of Ben, too, she thought, and her stomach twisted with love. He was a wonderful father.

They discharged Luke with a sharp lecture about the danger of swallowing things that weren't meant for him and Christy gave the mother a leaflet on preventing accidents in the home.

'Wow!' Billy's eyes were filled with admiration as he looked at her. 'I was just about to try and take blood from that child and I wasn't looking forward to it. What made you suspect that he hadn't swallowed them? It would never even have occurred to me.'

'Mother's instinct,' Christy said dryly, as she briskly tidied up the room ready for the next patient. 'Children often do unexpected things and his mother made that comment about hiding things.' She turned to Alessandro as Billy left the room. 'Do you remember Ben going through a phase of hiding everything?'

'Only too well.' Alessandro reached for the jacket that he'd abandoned. 'I seem to remember that he took my bleeper for twenty-four hours once.'

Christy grinned. 'I found it at the bottom of the laundry basket underneath a week's worth of dirty washing.'

Alessandro gave a nod and his eyes were

warm. 'You did well,' he said softly. 'Extremely well. Were it not for you, that child would now be undergoing some very unpleasant tests.'

'Well, they certainly would have put him off swallowing tablets that didn't belong to him.'

'You're an excellent A and E nurse,' Alessandro said quietly. 'I'd forgotten just how good and for that I apologise. It is where you are at your best and you should certainly not be wasting your talents anywhere else. You should come back.'

She stared at him for a long moment, her breath trapped in her lungs. What exactly was he saying? Come back to A and E or come back to him?

Their eyes locked and Christy felt warmth spread inside her. It was still there, she told herself. That special bond that had always existed between them. It hadn't died.

'Alessandro?' Katya's slender frame appeared round the door. Her hair was fastened on top of her head but several strands fell softly over her eyes, giving her a sleepy, sexy appearance. 'I'm going home now, but I'll see you at the Snow Ball tomorrow night. You owe me a dance.'

Christy felt the special warmth inside her evaporate, to be replaced by a block of ice.

Was that why he wanted to go to the Christmas party? Because Katya was going?

Telling herself that she was being paranoid, Christy turned her attention back to the state of the room, trying not to listen to Alessandro's response.

It didn't matter what he thought of Katya, she reminded herself, because she was going to buy a killer dress and remind him exactly what it was that he was missing.

CHAPTER SEVEN

'IT'S freezing today,' Christy turned round and looked at the children who were safely strapped into the back of the car as Alessandro drove the short distance to the forest. 'Did you two remember gloves and hats?'

'Stop fussing, Mum.' Katy yawned and Ben carried on playing with his space shuttle, lifting it into the air and making it swoop downwards.

'Yeeow-w-w…' he whined, flying it dangerously close to his sister's head.

Anticipating fireworks, Christy pointed out of the window. 'Oh, look, we're here.'

They climbed out of the car and the children hurried off to take a closer look at the trees.

'I like this one,' Ben yelled, and Katy rolled her eyes in derision.

'It's completely lopsided. This one is a much better shape.'

Ben frowned. 'Isn't.'

Alessandro strolled across to them and selected an entirely different tree. 'This one,' he said in his usual decisive fashion, and Christy smothered a smile.

Even with Christmas trees, he had to be the one in charge, but the children didn't seem to mind and jumped up and down with excitement as Alessandro paid and loaded it into the car.

Back home, Christy put mince pies in the oven to heat and dug out the boxes of decorations they'd used for years.

The children had put Christmas songs on the CD player and were dancing round the room, giggling and playing together.

Like any normal family, Christy thought as she handed another wooden reindeer to Ben to hang on the lower branches. Except they weren't a normal family. Did Alessandro love her? Did he want to fix their marriage or was this show of togetherness purely for the children? She didn't know and she was afraid to ask in case she heard something she didn't want to hear.

'Please, lift me so that I can do the fairy,' Katy demanded, and Christy gave a wan smile.

Like daughter, like father. Katy knew exactly what she wanted and was prepared to fight to get it.

She thought of the dress safely hidden at the back of her wardrobe.

It had cost a fortune, but if it helped remind Alessandro that she was more than the mother of his two children then it would have been worth the investment.

Alessandro scooped Katy up easily and held her while she carefully placed the sparkling fairy on top of the tree. Then he lowered her and dropped a kiss on her forehead.

He'd save their marriage for the sake of the children, Christy thought numbly, because he was an excellent father and adored them. But she wanted so much more than that. She wanted a return to the greedy, hungry passion that they'd always shared. Their relationship had been so unbelievably intense and special that it was hard to imagine settling for less.

Did he still love her?

Because she didn't want her children growing up witnessing a dead relationship.

She couldn't do it, she decided. She'd make one last attempt to fight for him and if it didn't work, they'd have to part.

She slipped away while Alessandro was reading to Ben, anxious to give herself plenty of time to get ready.

Remembering Katya's flawless appearance, she took extra time over her make-up and hair and finally slid into the dress.

Glancing in the mirror, she gave a soft, womanly smile. It was fabulous.

The dress was silver and the luxurious, unusual fabric shimmered and slid over her smooth curves.

'Not bad for someone of your age,' Katy murmured, walking into the room, sucking a lolly which she'd stolen from the Christmas tree. 'You need some diamonds to go with it. Something round your neck.'

Christy blinked. 'I haven't got anything suitable.'

Alessandro never bought her jewellery. It wasn't his style. She glanced down at the simple gold band on the ring finger of her left hand. They'd got married in such a hurry that they'd never even bothered with an engagement ring.

'Wait there.' Katy sprinted out of the room and came back carrying a silver necklace. 'Try that.'

'Where did you get it?'

Katy grinned and jumped onto the middle of the bed where she proceeded to sit, cross-legged. 'The front of a magazine, but don't worry about that. Fake is cool. Go for it, Mum.'

Laughing, Christy fastened the necklace around her throat and stood back to judge the effect. It was perfect. With a conspiratorial smile at her daughter, she slipped her feet into the extravagant strappy shoes she'd purchased and picked up her bag.

'Well? What's the verdict?'

'You look like something from the Christmas tree,' Ben breathed from the doorway. 'Like a real live princess.'

'Which has to be better than a dead princess,'

Katy said dryly, rolling her eyes and sliding off the bed. 'Come on. We'd better make sure Dad isn't planning on wearing that ribbed jumper he's been in all day.'

'I'm not wearing a jumper.' His voice deep and disturbingly masculine, Alessandro appeared in the doorway, dressed in a black dinner jacket that emphasised the width of his powerful shoulders.

He looked startlingly handsome and Christy caught her breath.

After all these years, she thought to herself, he still made her stare.

And he was staring, too.

His gaze slid from her eyes to her mouth, then lingered on the swell of her breasts revealed by the cut of the fabric and then finally rested on the hemline, which stopped a long way short of her knees.

'You're not going out like that.'

Poised for a compliment, Christy felt her happiness shatter. 'Sorry?'

'It isn't the sort of dress you should be wearing. It's revealing and it's—' Alessandro broke off, the expression in his eyes dark and dangerous as he struggled to find the right words. 'It's just not suitable.'

Christy felt her own temper rise.

The dress was perfect and she *knew* she looked fabulous. All day she'd been cocooned in the delicious anticipation of the moment when he saw her in the dress. And he'd spoiled it.

'Why isn't it suitable?'

Alessandro prowled around the room, his expression dark and ominous. 'You are a wife and a mother, and that dress makes you look like…' He inhaled sharply and stabbed long fingers through his hair, 'it makes you look like…'

'A woman?' Christy slotted in helpfully. 'You didn't think I could still work in A and E, but I've proved you wrong. You didn't think I could still be a useful member of the mountain rescue team, but I proved you wrong there, too. To you, I've ceased to be an individual. To you, I'm just a wife and a mother.' Her voice cracked as she said the words. 'But I've got news for you. Yes, I'm a wife and a mother, but I'm also a woman, Alessandro Garcia, and it's time you remembered that fact and stopped behaving like a caveman.'

Having delivered that speech, she walked from the room with as much dignity as she could muster, given the ridiculous height of the heels she'd chosen.

Alessandro stood in the centre of the room, his powerful shoulders rigid with tension as he struggled to control his simmering temper.

'Well…' His daughter's voice came from directly behind him. 'I'd say that you *really* messed that one up!'

Disturbed from his contemplation of that exact same fact, Alessandro rounded on his daughter with a growl. 'I did not ask for your opinion.'

'Maybe not, but I'm in this family, too!' Katy put her hands on her hips, her temper flaring as quickly as his. 'I don't see why I should have to sit around and watch the two of you ruin everything. Mum bought a new dress and she looks nice—for an older person,' she added quickly as an afterthought, and Alessandro frowned.

'Your mother is only thirty-two.'

'Is she *that* old?' Katy shuddered and pulled a face. 'Hard to imagine.'

At any other time Alessandro would have laughed but he was too busy contemplating the facts to respond to the horror in his daughter's expression.

Thirty-two. Many women weren't even married at that age, he mused. Christy was still young. He'd met her young and made her pregnant almost immediately.

And his daughter was right. She had looked nice in the dress. More than nice. Gorgeous. Sexy. Stunning.

Closing his eyes to clear the image of long slender legs and tempting feminine curves, he realised that Christy had been spot on in her accusation. He was behaving like a caveman. The truth was that he didn't want any other man admiring what was his. Especially at the moment, when their relationship was so precarious.

She'd given no indication as to what was going to happen when Christmas was over. Hadn't mentioned whether she was staying or going, and he was afraid to ask in case his question provoked her into leaving.

He felt as though he was totally out of step with her thinking.

She confided in Jake, it seemed, but not him.

He inhaled sharply. Jake. He knew only too well that Jake had been crazy about Christy for a short time. Given the complexity and number of Jake's subsequent relationships, he'd assumed that the connection had long since died. Now he was starting to wonder…

But no matter what, she was right about his behaviour, he reflected with grim self-awareness. He'd behaved that way from the first moment he'd met her. She'd been twenty and a virgin, and he'd fallen for her so hard that, given the choice, he would have locked her inside a room and never let her out.

She'd been with him for almost all of her adult life.

Could he blame her if she now wanted to dress up and party?

He ran a hand over the back of his neck and cursed fluently in Spanish.

Katy cleared her throat. 'Thanks to those boring Spanish lessons I endure every Saturday morning, I understood that,' she said calmly, and Alessandro threw her a quelling look.

'I don't need your comments at this time,' he said in Spanish, and she gave a smile and responded in the same language.

'Oh, I rather think you do.'

So much for expecting Alessandro to sweep her into his arms, Christy thought miserably as she reached for her coat. He hadn't seen her as an attractive woman. Just as his wife, inappropriately dressed.

Part of her wanted to strip off the dress and have an early night in the spare room, regardless of the broken bed, but part of her was still determined to show him what he was missing, so she picked up the phone and called a taxi.

Alessandro strode into the hall moments later. 'Christy—'

'We need to leave,' she said coldly, not giving him the chance to say what she would undoubtedly consider to be the wrong thing. 'I ordered a taxi so that we can both have a drink. It should be here any minute.'

Alessandro inhaled sharply. '*Por Dios*, we need to talk.'

'About what?' She swept towards the door, her head held high, her hair streaming down her back like flames. 'The fact that you don't see me as anything other than the mother of your children? You've made that perfectly clear, Alessandro. I don't need you to labour the point.'

She yanked open the front door, relieved to see the taxi arrive.

They made the journey to the manor house that was the venue for the Snow Ball in tense, brooding silence, and Christy turned her head to stare out of the window, afraid to look at him.

Afraid that she'd break down.

Merry Christmas, Christy, she thought bitterly as the taxi swept up the wide, snowy drive that led to the stately home. Christmas trees festooned with tiny lights adorned the entrance but she decided that it was impossible to be enchanted when your marriage was on the rocks.

Determined not to show Alessandro how much

his casual indifference had hurt her, Christy handed her coat to the uniformed attendant and walked into the ballroom.

The party was already in full swing, the dance floor was crowded and the buffet table was loaded with festive food.

Huge boughs of holly and mistletoe decorated the room and the air was filled with the scent of pine cones and fir trees.

Christmas.

Christy blinked back tears. It should have been a happy time.

The first person she saw was Nicky, wearing a slinky green dress and clinging to her husband's arm. 'Christy!' Waving a champagne glass, she sprinted over and embraced her. 'You look amazing!'

At least someone thought so, Christy thought sadly, forcing a smile. 'Thanks.'

Nicky grinned at Alessandro. 'She looks unbelievably sexy, doesn't she?'

Alessandro's already black expression darkened still further and Christy quickly made conversation to cover his lack of response.

Clearly he didn't find her sexy.

'Come and dance,' Nicky urged, and Christy nodded.

'Great idea.' Anything was better than standing with Alessandro. He obviously didn't want her to go out. Didn't want her to have a good time and enjoy herself.

She walked towards the dance floor with Nicky and let herself go.

For a short time she blocked out everything except the rhythm of the music and the feel of her own body.

Eventually heat and thirst got the better of her and she helped herself to a drink and walked outside into the grounds for some fresh air.

The snow was thick on the ground and she suddenly wished she'd asked for her coat.

Turning to go back inside, she bumped straight into Jake. 'Well, well, Cinderella, I assume,' he drawled in a soft voice, and she smiled.

'Hi, there. Where's your date?'

'Not sure.' Jake glanced back at the house and frowned. 'In there somewhere. Last seen throwing herself around the dance floor in a most embarrassing fashion. Time to move on to the next candidate, I think.'

Christy rolled her eyes. 'You're irrepressible.'

'No, I'm just fussy,' Jake said calmly, his eyes on her pale face. Without commenting, he shrugged out of his jacket and slipped it around her shoulders. 'OK, what's happening with you?'

The jacket was warm and comforting but she frowned. 'You'll freeze.'

'Me? You're forgetting that I'm big, tough and manly.' Jake lifted her chin and forced her to look at him. 'Come one. What's happened?'

She shouldn't say anything, she thought miserably. She ought to keep her problems to herself. 'Nothing.'

'Christy, we need to get to the point fast, before we both catch pneumonia,' Jake said patiently, 'so let's put this another way. Why are you out here on your own, leaving your husband inside and fair game for that Russian doctor with the long claws and the evil eyes.'

'Katya?' Christy swallowed hard. So Jake had noticed, too. 'I can't compete with her.'

'That's rubbish,' Jake drawled, finishing his

drink and putting his glass down on the wall that led towards the maze. 'I thought you were going to fight.'

'I was.' Christy looked down at herself. 'This was my weapon, but it didn't work. He was supposed to be bowled over by how stunning I am. Instead, he just went off the deep end and said that I couldn't go out looking like this.'

Jake's eyes narrowed. 'Is that right?'

'I'm the mother of his children,' Christy said wearily, and Jake grinned.

'In that silver dress? Believe me, you look more like a walking fantasy than the mother of anyone's children. I'm not surprised he didn't want you to go out looking like that. He has a possessive nature, angel. And that's your fault for marrying a brooding Spaniard. You should have picked someone safe and English, like me.'

'You're wrong. If it was about feeling possessive, he would have grabbed me and we never would have made it to the party,' Christy said miserably. 'But he doesn't want me.'

'No?' Jake lifted his eyes from hers and looked over her shoulder, his attention caught by something directly behind her. She saw his expression change but before she could turn and see what he was looking at, he muttered something that sounded like, 'Oh, what the hell', dragged her against him and brought his mouth down hard on hers.

The kiss lasted less than a few seconds because suddenly Jake was yanked away from her so violently that she almost lost her balance.

'Get your hands *off* my wife,' Alessandro growled fiercely, his powerful body pulsing with vibrant energy and barely contained tension.

Christy swallowed. 'Alessandro—'

He didn't glance in her direction. 'Do not speak to me at the moment,' he said thickly, his voice raw with aggression. 'This is not your fault. You're inexperienced when it comes to men, but Jake is—'

'Yes?' Jake looked at him calmly, his hands in his pockets. 'What am I?'

'You've always wanted her,' Alessandro breathed with icy fury, and Jake gave a curious smile.

'Yes. I did.'

'*Por Dios*, you admit it?' Like a tiger suddenly

unleashed, Alessandro stepped forward and let out a punch that sent Jake flying into the snow.

'Jake!' Christy gave a scream of horror and ran towards him. 'Alessandro, no! Stop it. Stop it now! I can't believe you just did that! What do you think you're *doing*?'

'Protecting what's mine.' Alessandro was nursing his hand, his eyes still glittering with fury as he watched Jake struggle to his feet and lift a hand to his split lip.

Christy was forgotten as the two men faced each other.

'I guess I deserved that,' Jake said softly, 'but you're only allowed the one, Garcia. And now you'd better let me finish my sentence. It's true that I wanted Christy when I thought she was available. Unfortunately that lasted all of twenty-four hours. Then she saw you and I didn't get a look-in. You were the only man for her. You still are, but you're too pig-headed to see it.'

Seeing blood on his chin, Christy took a step towards him but Jake lifted a hand to stop her. 'I'm fine. I'm going inside now to find my date. There's nothing like the sight of blood to bring out a woman's nurturing instincts.' Despite the bruise on his face, he gave her a saucy wink. 'I'll have the jacket back next time I see you, angel.'

She watched as he sauntered away, tears in her eyes. Then she turned to Alessandro in a state of appalled frustration. 'I can't *believe* you just did that. He's our oldest friend!'

'He was kissing you.'

'Well, at least he noticed me,' she yelled, 'which is more than you ever do.'

'I notice you.' Strong fingers closed around her wrist and he dragged her towards the entrance of the maze.

'Alessandro, this is ridiculous.' She tugged at her hand but he kept on walking until they reached the walled garden in the centre of the maze. A fountain bubbled and the moon shed just enough light for her to be able to make out the hard, unyielding expression on his handsome face. Soft flakes of snow swirled around them but both were oblivious to everything except each other and the steadily mounting tension.

'You think I don't notice you, *querida*?' He backed her against the wall, his powerful body hard against hers, his hand on her waist. 'You think I'm not aware of you lying next to me in bed at night? *You think I don't notice the silver dress?*'

Hunger exploded inside her and she clung to the front of his jacket, the intimate thrust of his body sending her pulse rate skyward.

He jerked the hem of her dress upwards and she gave a soft gasp of shock and excitement as she felt the strength of his hands on her bottom. 'Well, I've got news for you, *gatita*, I notice.' He brought his mouth down on hers in a hard, possessive kiss and she melted under the skilled seduction of his mouth.

No one kissed like Alessandro, she thought dizzily as she felt herself go under, sucked down into a sensual world where everything was suddenly hazy.

Her heart thumped, hot tongues of fire licked deep inside her and she slid her arms round his strong neck and held onto his head just in case he had any intention of ending the kiss before she was ready.

But clearly he didn't.

Without lifting his mouth, he slid his hands

inside the silk of her panties and the warmth of his palms was such a contrast to the freezing night air that she gasped against his lips and then cried out his name as his fingers slid inside her, exploring the most intimate place of all.

He was the only man who had ever touched her that way and she felt her body explode with an excitement so intense that it was close to unbearable.

'I want you,' he groaned huskily, lifting her with a powerful movement and anchoring her between the wall and his body, *'Por Dios*, I have to have you now. I can't wait any longer.'

Exulting in the effect she was having on him, Christy wrapped her legs around him, desperate for him to finish what he'd started, desperate to ease the agonising ache that built deep inside her body. And still they kissed, as if they were never going to stop.

As if this were the last time they would ever touch.

In a swift movement that said a great deal about his physical strength, Alessandro held her secure with one arm and then reached down to deal with the zip of his trousers. Breathless with anticipation, she felt him hard and ready against her and shifted her hips with a whimper of need as the white-hot burning low in her pelvis reached almost intolerable levels.

He held her firm and entered her with a powerful thrust and she gasped against his mouth as she felt the slick, velvety thickness of his arousal deep inside her.

She forgot everything except the ferocious needs of her own body and his. She forgot that they were outdoors. She forgot the freezing cold air and the sharp, uneven surface of the bricks pressing into her back. *She forgot that their marriage was in crisis.*

Her entire focus was the building, throbbing ache that grew and grew deep inside her.

He was hard and demanding, his mouth never leaving hers, each rhythmic thrust creating erotic sensations that bordered on the painful. She tried desperately to move her hips, to alleviate the frantic ache deep in her body but he controlled her utterly and she gave a sob of relief as she felt him change the angle and drive her towards the edge.

She toppled with a force that shocked her and she clung to his broad shoulders, feeling his body tense as he drove still deeper into her and fell with her.

And finally, when their breathing had calmed and their pulses had slowed, he lifted his head and lowered her gently to the ground.

For a moment they both stared at each other, connected by the unique intensity of the experience that they'd shared.

No other man would ever make her feel like this, she thought dreamily as she stared up at him, still holding his arms for support. *No other man.*

And then he reached forward, straightened her dress and rescued Jake's jacket, which had fallen to the ground.

He placed it gently round her shoulders, his dark gaze lingering on her face with brooding intensity.

And she waited.

Waited to hear him say the words she was longing to hear. *I love you.*

Surely he was going to say it any moment now. After what they'd just shared, how could he say anything else? What other words would possibly be appropriate in this situation?

Everything was going to be all right.

This was going to be a new beginning for them.

He grasped the lapels of the jacket and hauled her against him, moulding her against his lean, powerful frame with a strength that made her gasp.

'You're mine,' he groaned, burying his face in her neck and trailing burning kisses over her bare skin. 'Mine and no other man's.'

Rigid with pent-up emotions and expecting an entirely different declaration, Christy froze. 'I'm sorry?' Her voice croaky, she pulled away from him, a warning flash in her eyes. Had she heard him correctly? 'Say that again?'

'We belong together—and I *won't* give you a divorce.'

Deciding that this wasn't the time to point out that she'd never actually asked him for a divorce, Christy felt all the soft feelings melt away. 'Is that was this was all about? You make love to me for the first time in more than two months and you do it as a gesture of *possession*?'

Immediately on the defensive, Alessandro's dark eyes narrowed warily. 'Of course not…'

But suddenly Christy was able to see the whole

picture with an uncomfortable degree of clarity. 'Until Jake kissed me, you didn't lay a finger on me. You did it because he kissed me.'

He tensed. 'I'm allowed to make love to my wife.'

'I've been lying half-naked next to you in bed for the past week,' she said through gritted teeth, 'and you haven't laid a finger on me. It doesn't take a genius to understand that Jake was the reason you just ripped my clothes off in a public place in below freezing weather conditions. Permit me to tell you that I find your romantic streak less than impressive.'

'I just made love to you.'

'No, Alessandro,' she snapped, her delicate chin jerking upwards and her eyes flashing with anger. 'You just had sex with me. Sex, designed to stake your claim and wipe all thoughts of other men from my mind.'

A muscle worked in his lean jaw and his eyes gleamed dark as he lifted his head in an arrogant gesture. 'And it worked—tell me you can feel that with any other man and I will know you're lying.'

Goaded beyond reason, she lifted a hand and slapped him hard.

'You may be a brilliant doctor, Alessandro Garcia,' she choked, 'but you're a tactless, thoughtless, possessive ba—' She stopped herself before she could say the word she wanted to say, her upbringing preventing her from giving voice to a word that she'd never before had reason to use.

It was bad enough that she'd hit him when she'd never before struck anyone or anything.

If she'd needed the evidence that he didn't love her, she had it now, she thought miserably as she turned and stumbled down the path that led out of the maze

He didn't love her but he didn't want any other man to have her.

And she couldn't see a future for their marriage.

Simmering with barely contained frustration, and cursing the inconsistencies of the female sex, Alessandro strode out of the maze after Christy, only to see her long, gorgeous legs folding into the back of a taxi, which promptly disappeared down the snowy drive.

He cursed in Spanish and then turned to find Jake watching him. His eyes narrowed with accusation. 'Did *you* put her in a cab?'

'Why?' Jake's tone was cool. 'Are you going to punch me again?'

'No.' Alessandro ran a hand over the back of his neck. 'Providing you don't kiss her again. Ever.'

'I thought it might wake you up.' Jake rubbed a hand over his bruised jaw. 'I think it worked.'

Alessandro shot him an incredulous look. 'I think you like to live dangerously. I wanted to kill you with my bare hands.'

'I hoped it would be enough to galvanise you into action and show her what you felt about her, but, judging from the tears on her face when I got her the taxi, you didn't succeed.'

'Tears?' Alessandro digested that unwelcome piece of news and inhaled sharply. 'Christy *never* cries.'

'Well, she was crying just now,' Jake said flatly, his gaze steady as he looked at his friend. 'What did you do to her?'

A tinge of colour touched Alessandro's hard cheekbones. 'I made love to her,' he growled finally, 'which seemed like the right thing to do at the time.'

Jake studied him. 'Judging from the mark on your cheek, I'm guessing it wasn't.'

'Women are *totally* incomprehensible.'

'Are they?' Jake met his gaze head on, ignoring the snow settling on his white shirt. 'Christy doesn't believe you love her any more, Al.'

'She doesn't think I love her?' Alessandro's voice rang with exasperation. 'She's the one who left the family home, taking the children with her.'

'She expected you to follow her.'

Alessandro stared at him blankly. 'You're wrong. If she'd wanted me to follow her, why did she leave in the first place? And if that was true, why didn't she just come back straight away? It doesn't make sense.'

'That's because you're looking at it from a man's point of view. She was waiting for a sign that you still cared. She didn't think you loved her any more.'

Alessandro gritted his teeth. 'If that's true, making love to her should have proved otherwise. But she's just hit me and left in a taxi.'

Jake sighed. 'I think your timing might have been a bit out. If you'd made your move at any point before I'd kissed her, you'd probably be snuggled up together now, with this whole nightmarish episode behind you.'

Alessandro's eyes darkened ominously. 'I do *not* want to be reminded that you kissed my wife, Blackwell.'

'You're the one she wants,' Jake said calmly, 'but you're making such a mess of it you're going to lose her if you're not careful.'

Lose her?

Lose Christy?

Faced with that unthinkable possibility, Alessandro felt helpless for the first time in his life. 'What do I do?' His voice was hoarse. 'What do I do to convince her that I love her?'

'Try telling her.'

'She won't believe me after tonight.'

'Then show her,' Jake said quietly. 'Show her that you love her, Al, but do it fast.'

CHAPTER EIGHT

INSUFFERABLE, arrogant, miserable, vile, arrogant rat. Christy flung clothes into the suitcase, her face streaked with tears as she lengthened her list of possible adjectives to apply to Alessandro.

And as for herself—she gave a growl of exasperation and flung a skirt violently into the case. Then she sat on the edge of the bed and buried her face in her hands with a groan of humiliation and self-disgust.

Did she have no self-control?

When she thought about the way she'd behaved she just wanted to curl up and die on the spot.

He didn't love her at all and yet she'd thrown herself at him like a desperate, sex-starved groupie. She'd virtually *begged*, for goodness' sake, and all in a place where anyone could have come past and seen them at any point.

How embarrassing was *that*?

What had possessed her to behave like that?

It was true that she and Alessandro had always been very physically compatible, but they'd always kept their passion for each other behind closed doors.

Tonight she'd thought about nothing except the desperate need to have him make love to her. And for her it had all been about love.

Whereas he'd thought about nothing but possession.

With a sniff and a determined lift of her chin, she stood up and turned back to the case and then froze when she saw Alessandro standing in the doorway.

His glossy hair was dusted with snow and his dark jaw shadowed by stubble. At some point— had it been before or after they'd had sex?—he'd undone his bow-tie and it was now draped carelessly around his neck, the open collar of his shirt revealing a tantalising hint of bronzed skin and curling dark body hair. 'You're *not* leaving.'

She closed her eyes to block out the vision of perfect masculinity. 'This is never going to work, Alessandro. I'm going to sleep at my mother's tonight.'

She didn't trust herself to behave normally in front of the children.

He didn't love her. He saw her as a possession and the mother of his children. Not as a woman.

'It's worked for the past twelve years.' He kicked the door shut behind him and she opened her eyes, startled by the raw pain she saw in his dark eyes.

'Alessandro—'

'I told myself that if you loved Jake then I'd let you go, but now I find that I can't do that.'

She gaped at him. 'I *don't* love Jake.'

'You were kissing him. You're always confiding in him.'

'He was kissing me,' she corrected swiftly, 'and I confide in him because he listens.'

Alessandro's eyes darkened. 'And I don't?'

'Well, no.' She refused to be intimidated by the black expression on his face. 'No, you don't. You never show any interest in me as a woman any more.'

He sucked in a long breath. 'I admit that I may have made mistakes in our relationship.' He jerked his bow-tie from his neck and flung it onto the bed. 'But I think I at least deserve another chance.'

She stared at him. 'Was that an apology?' In twelve years she'd never known Alessandro apologise for anything. 'Are you actually admitting that you might be in the wrong?'

He took a deep breath. 'You should *not* have left and taken the children,' he growled, 'but, yes, I'm willing to admit that my behaviour may have fallen short of perfect.'

She wanted to laugh. As far as apologies went it was pretty pathetic, but for Alessandro it was a major step forward.

She dropped the suitcase on the floor of the bedroom. 'So what are you suggesting?'

His jacket joined the bow tie on the bed. 'Christmas is a week away. I want us to try again—we owe it to the children.'

Was that why he was doing this? Was it all about the children?

'All right.' Her heart was thudding. 'But there are rules.'

'Rules?'

'I carry on working in A and E and I go out with the mountain rescue team and you stop frowning and glaring at me—'

'I don't frown and glare.'

'You frown and glare.'

'All right.' His voice was rough. 'I'll try not to. You're an excellent A and E nurse. I don't know how I could have forgotten that. This last week has been easier for everyone because you've been in the department. I'm certainly not going to suggest that you give it up.'

'Oh.' A delicious warmth spread through her and she stared at him, stunned by the praise.

He lifted a dark eyebrow in question. 'Anything else?'

'Yes. If I'm staying, then we're going to spend time together, Alessandro. No more ships in the night. No more living at the hospital while I live my own life here. And a few romantic gestures would be nice.'

'Romantic gestures?' He stared at her blankly for a moment and she resisted the temptation to roll her eyes.

'Never mind. Let's just settle for spending time

together,' she said wearily, lacking the motivation to explain. Romantic gestures just weren't in his nature, she reminded herself. She'd known that when she'd married him and it hadn't bothered her. She'd been in love with the man and she was still in love with him. If they could just rediscover what they'd once shared, she could live without romantic gestures.

There was a brief silence while he studied her and then he gave a brief nod. 'All right. Agreed. I have only one rule.'

Christy looked at him, her eyes wide. 'You do?'

'No more kissing,' Alessandro delivered softly, strolling towards her with a strange gleam in his eyes. 'Unless it's me.'

He was close to her now, so close that she could almost feel the heat of his powerful body, and the breath was suddenly trapped in her throat. 'I didn't kiss him.'

'Good.' Alessandro's voice was a low, lethal purr. 'Because I don't share. *Ever.*'

The sexual tension between them was stifling. 'You're behaving like a caveman again.'

'A very restrained caveman,' Alessandro pointed out in silky tones, his mouth hovering dangerously close to hers. 'So far I haven't locked the door, thrown you on the bed or done any of the things I'm burning to do. In fact, *gatita*, I'm showing remarkable self-control.'

She waited for him to kiss her but instead he studied her for a long, lingering moment, the expression in his eyes partially screened by thick, dark lashes. Then he stepped back and walked towards the shower.

'Don't wait up for me,' he drawled as he ripped off the white shirt and dropped it in the vague vicinity of the laundry basket. 'I'm sure you're tired.'

Don't wait up for him?

Christy stared at him in disbelief and mounting frustration as he strolled into the *en suite* bathroom and casually pushed the door shut behind him.

He'd had wild, abandoned sex with her just because another man had kissed her but now, when he'd declared his intention of making their marriage work, he strolled into the bathroom without laying a single finger on her.

What was the matter with the man?

* * *

Romantic gestures?

What did she mean, he never made romantic gestures?

Alessandro hit the buttons on the shower and brooded on the mysteries of the female sex. He'd just made love to her. *How much more romantic than that could a man get?* And yet she'd accused him of being possessive.

Only a desire to avoid similar confrontation had prevented him from stripping her naked and taking her to bed to finish what they'd started at the Snow Ball.

But he wasn't going to touch her, he reminded himself, turning the shower to cold to help his resolve.

She'd said that they didn't spend enough time together so he'd correct that. And he'd make so many romantic gestures that she wouldn't be able to turn around without falling over one.

Once he found out what they were…

The following day Christy found herself working alongside Jake, who had been called down to look at a young woman who was bleeding.

'Ouch.' Her voice was soft as her eyes rested on his bruised mouth. 'That looks sore.'

'It's more embarrassing than sore,' Jake drawled, touching his fingers to his lips with a wry smile. 'The entire hospital seem to be laying bets on whose wife I seduced last night.'

Christy blushed. 'Did you tell them the truth?'

Jake lifted an eyebrow. 'What do you think?'

'I think you're much too good a friend to gossip,' she said quietly, 'and I'm really grateful for that. And for lots of other things.'

He studied her for a moment and then smiled and held out his hand for the notes she was holding. 'So—where's this woman you want me to see?'

'In cubicle one. I'll act as chaperone.'

The day passed swiftly and Christy was just wondering how she'd managed to miss yet another lunch-break when the ambulance hotline rang.

She picked up the phone just as Alessandro strolled up to her. 'Tonight,' he said in a decisive tone. 'We're going out to dinner. I've booked a table for eight o'clock.'

In no position to argue, Christy spoke into the phone and listened while the ambulance gave the details of a casualty they were bringing in.

She scribbled a few notes, replaced the phone and discovered that he was still standing there. 'They're bringing in a fifty-five-year-old man with an upper GI bleed. Apparently he vomited up fresh blood about half an hour ago.'

Alessandro's gaze lingered on her face. 'Then we'd better call the physicians and warn them. You're thinking that I won't make that date of ours tonight, aren't you?'

'Well, I...' The words died in her mouth as she caught his slow, sexy smile.

'Be ready, Christy,' he said softly, 'because I'm going to be there.'

Her stomach turned over and she cursed herself for being so weak-willed. It was going to take more than one evening where he happened to show up to fix their marriage.

The patient arrived accompanied by sirens and clutching a vomit bowl filled with frank blood.

Christy snapped on a pair of gloves and an apron and helped the paramedics transfer him to the trolley.

'This is Duncan Finn.' The paramedic removed the red blanket covering his patient and Christy substituted one of the department's own. 'Suddenly started vomiting and noticed the blood.'

Katya slid into the room just as Alessandro moved round the trolley to talk to his patient.

'Any history of abdominal pain, Mr Finn?' he asked smoothly, as he swiftly examined the contents of the bowl and then picked up the patient's wrist to check his pulse and capillary refill.

The patient shook his head and Alessandro methodically ran through a list of questions as he continued his examination.

'Shall I put a line in?' Katya asked, and Alessandro gave a nod.

'Two. Christy will show you which cannula.'

Christy pushed forward the trolley that she'd already prepared and handed the other doctor a tourniquet.

'I want a full blood count, a clotting screen, U and Es, blood glucose and group and cross-match. Christy…' he lifted his head from his examination '…what are his sats?'

'Ninety-six per cent,' she said immediately, and he gave a nod.

'Did you bleep the physicians?'

'As the ambulance arrived.' Seeing that Katya had successfully cannulated the patient, Christy handed her the right bottles for the various tests and labelled the necessary forms. 'They said that they were on their way.'

'I want him to have 50 grams ranitidine, diluted in saline.' Alessandro's eyes rested on the monitor. 'Let's give him some oxygen, Christy.'

Murmuring words of reassurance to her patient, Christy slipped a mask over his face and adjusted the flow.

'I'm so thirsty,' he mumbled. 'Can I have a drink?'

'Nothing at the moment,' Christy said, and at that moment the physicians arrived.

Having made their examination and listened to Alessandro's handover, they decided that the patient needed an endoscopy and made arrangements to take him to Theatre.

Christy arranged the transfer, accompanied the

patient and then returned to Resus to tidy up the mess she'd left.

Pushing open the door, she was surprised to find Alessandro and Katya still in there, talking.

Katya was standing quite close to him, closer than was strictly necessary, her eyes fixed on Alessandro's face.

'So you're saying that the differential diagnosis could have been a Mallory-Weiss tear, oesophageal varices, some sort of mucosal inflammation, gastric carcinoma or a coagulation disorder.'

'It could also have been a simple peptic ulcer,' Alessandro said dryly, dropping his gloves into the nearest bin. 'Not everything we see in this department is rare or out of the ordinary. Remember that.'

'Of course,' Katya breathed. 'I hope you don't mind me taking the opportunity to ask questions.'

'Not at all.' Watching Alessandro's encouraging smile, Christy ground her teeth.

He was *so* patient with her. Why was that? Patience wasn't one of his virtues.

'Do you fancy a drink tonight, Alessandro?

I could really do with your help on a few issues,' Katya murmured, and Christy watched as her husband gave the younger girl a thoughtful look.

'Unfortunately tonight isn't possible,' he said, his Spanish accent very pronounced as he reached for a pen to sign a request form that one of the nurses was holding out to him. 'Some other time maybe.'

Some other time?

The hairs on the back of Christy's neck prickled with outrage. What did he mean by that? Why some other time? And exactly what sort of help was Katya looking for?

Ready to hit him for the second time in twenty-four hours, Christy cleared the trolley noisily and slammed her foot on the bar that opened the bin. It gaped open and she stuffed in the rubbish and let it slam shut with a crash.

Not very mature, she thought to herself, but at least it made her feel better and it reminded the pair of them that she was in the room.

He had such a nerve!

First he had hit Jake for kissing her and now he was flirting with Katya.

Aware that Alessandro was looking at her with astonishment, she gave him an innocent smile. 'Well, that's just about finished with the clearing up. I'll be off, then, and leave you to it.'

His eyes narrowed. 'Leave us to what?'

Despite her clenched jaw, she managed to beam at him. 'To whatever it is you have to do, Alessandro,' she replied in perfect Spanish, and then turned and left the room.

By the time she arrived home, she'd made up her mind that Alessandro was going to be staying at the hospital so what was the point of changing for dinner? Still seething about the sheer front of the feline Katya, she stepped into the shower, wondering how Alessandro had dealt with her.

Were they together at this precise moment?

Was he giving her personal instruction?

Still simmering, Christy wrapped herself in a large towel and padded into the bedroom, only to find him standing there holding a huge bunch of red roses.

She stared. 'What are those for?'

'They're for you.'

'Me?' He was giving her flowers? Alessandro never gave her flowers. It just wasn't something he thought to do. So why was he thinking of it now?

Her heart plummeted and she wondered again just what sort of help he'd been giving the seductive Katya. 'Feeling guilty about something, Alessandro?' Her frosty tone brought a wary look to his eyes.

He muttered something under his breath in Spanish and she glared at him.

'You *never* bring me flowers.'

'An omission which I'm trying to rectify,' he announced in a tone that reflected no small degree of exasperation and bemusement. 'You wanted me to be more romantic, *gatita*.'

She clutched at the towel, her hair trailing over her shoulders like flames. 'You think it's romantic to see my husband flirting under my nose?'

His eyes narrowed. '*When* was I flirting?'

'You really need to ask?' She flung her head back and her eyes sparked. 'She's all over you like a rash.'

'Who is?'

'Katya.' Christy hated her waspish tone and Alessandro lifted an eyebrow.

'Are you accusing me of having an affair with Katya?' His slow, masculine drawl was laced with amusement and she glared at the flowers and then at him, furious that he dared to laugh at her!

'Why is that funny?'

'She works for me, it is my job to train her,' Alessandro said smoothly, and Christy clenched her fists.

'And you have to be in close physical contact to achieve that objective?' She knew she was behaving childishly but she just couldn't help it.

'You are being ridiculous.'

'Am I?' Christy tilted her head in challenge. 'Last night you punched Jake.'

'That was entirely different,' Alessandro growled, the amusement in his eyes vanishing in a flash. 'He was kissing you.'

'And Katya was rubbing herself against you like a cat.' She broke off and Alessandro sucked in a breath, his gaze suddenly thoughtful.

'And you minded about that,' he said softly, 'so that's good, is it not?'

'Why would that *possibly* be good?'

'Jealousy shows that feeling exists.'

Did it? Did he still have feelings for her? Or were his feelings all linked with his traditional, Mediterranean man's view of family?

'You didn't think it was such a good thing last night when you split Jake's lip,' she pointed out, and Alessandro gave a wry smile.

'Good point. OK.' He gave a shrug of his broad shoulders that reflected his Latin heritage. 'So we both admit we are hot-tempered and foolish and then you put my flowers in water and we go out to dinner.' His sudden unexpected smile was so sexy and charismatic that she felt her stomach flip.

It had always been the same, she reflected weakly. One moment he was all seething, masculine volatility and the next all indolent, simmering sexuality.

'Are you trying to talk me round?'

'Perhaps.' His voice was a lazy drawl as he slipped a firm hand round the back of her neck and trailed his fingers slowly through her hair.

'Or perhaps we have done enough talking for one evening, *querida*. What do you think?'

She couldn't think at all with him looking down at her with that slightly teasing, sexy gleam in his dark eyes.

'I— We—' She didn't finish her sentence because he brought his mouth down on hers with passionate force, drugging her with the intensity of his kiss. She felt the strength in her knees dissolve and clutched at his broad shoulders for support.

And then he lifted his head, his gaze slumberous as he studied her face. 'On second thoughts, let's go out to dinner.'

She stared at him dizzily, her vision slightly hazy. 'Sorry?'

'If we stay here, I will seduce you,' he declared without a trace of apology, 'and then you might accuse me of being possessive or not being interested in you as a person. I hate the thought that Jake knows more about you than I do so I'm going to take you out and you are going to tell me everything.'

She almost laughed. It was typical of Alessandro to try and command a conversation. But at least he was trying. 'All right,' she said softly, basking in the masculine appreciation she saw in his eyes. 'Let's go out and I'll tell you everything.'

He took her to a tiny restaurant by the side of the lake and they sat at a secluded table festively decorated with bunches of holly.

Alessandro picked up a menu and ordered and then looked at her with a wary expression on his handsome face. 'Why are you looking at me like that?'

'Do you realise that you never let me order my own food?'

'All right.' He leaned back in his chair and gave a shrug. 'What would you have ordered?'

'Smoked salmon and duck.'

He gave an arrogant smile. 'So— I ordered you smoked salmon and duck. That makes me a genius, no?'

'It makes you controlling, Alessandro.'

He frowned. 'It means I know you well.'

'It means you don't even give me the choice.'

He let out a long breath and reached for his wine. 'OK.' Suddenly his Spanish accent sounded very pronounced. 'So from now on, you want to order your own food. No problem.'

She hesitated. 'It's not just my food, Alessandro, it's everything. I want to know that you care about my opinion. About me as a person.'

'Of course I care about you as a person.'

'And yet you didn't want me to work in A and E.'

'I was wrong in that,' he conceded. 'You have proved that you are still an excellent A and E nurse. Obviously you should be working in that area, not wasting your talents as a practice nurse. We will sort out a contract that allows you to be home for the children and work in the department.'

'You're doing it again!' She stared at him in exasperation. 'You're telling me what I should do. Try *asking* me, Alessandro. Try *asking* me what I want. Believe it or not, I have an opinion, too.'

He muttered something in Spanish and sat back as their first course arrived. 'All right.' He paused while the waiter placed the plates in front of him and then gave her a smile. 'I am asking you what you want. Tell me.'

'I want to make my own choices,' she said

softly. 'I want to decide what's right for me as well as for the family. Yes, I want to be there for the children, of course I do. If anything, it's even more important now they're getting older and they have homework to do and friends to play with, but I can easily combine that with work and the mountain rescue team.'

Alessandro picked up his fork. 'I want to know why you find Jake easy to talk to and not me.' A strange expression flickered in his dark eyes. 'Am I that intimidating?'

'Not to me,' she said quietly, 'but you're very self-confident and sure of yourself. And sometimes your confidence drives everything else along in its path. You're very strong and you make decisions for people.'

He studied her through narrowed eyes. 'But I have always been the same, I think.'

She gave a soft smile. 'Yes, you have.'

'You remember the first time we met?'

Colour flooded into her cheeks. 'I'm not likely to forget.'

'You were talking to Jake in the students' bar,' Alessandro said softly, 'and I took one look at you and knew then that you were going to be mine.'

'You grabbed me by the hand and dragged me across the road to that little restaurant—'

'And then you came back to my place,' Alessandro said in a deep, sexy drawl. 'And we didn't get out of bed for three days.'

Her colour deepened. 'I got pregnant that weekend.'

'And I was so pleased,' Alessandro confessed with a complete lack of remorse. 'It gave me a reason to marry you without having to suffer a long engagement.'

She stared down at the simple gold band on the finger of her left hand. At the time, getting engaged hadn't seemed to matter. She'd been swept away by the force of his passion and the intensity of her love for him.

And that love had deepened over the years as she'd discovered what an amazing man he was.

But how had he felt about her? Had the novelty worn off? 'All the women were after you.'

'But I wanted only you.'

And how about now? she wanted to ask. *How*

about now? Had he grown bored with the person she was? But she didn't want to risk spoiling a nice evening by hearing something she didn't want to hear and he was so obviously trying hard to listen to and understand her that she didn't want to threaten the atmosphere.

'It is true I am a strong person and that characteristic isn't helped by the job I do,' Alessandro confessed, disarmingly honest. 'In A and E, I don't operate by consensus. I am not going to stand there with an injured patient and ask everyone for an opinion on the correct treatment protocol. I am used to making snap decisions.'

And those snap decisions saved lives on a daily basis, Christy knew that. He was an incredibly skilled and talented doctor and his decisiveness and confidence was an important contributing factor in his success.

'When people have a tricky patient, they always want you there,' she said quietly, knowing that it was true. 'You never panic.'

'Panicking helps no one.' Alessandro reached for a bread roll. 'And confidence is important to everyone.'

Christy knew that to be true also. It was important to have someone competent in control. 'If I had an accident, there's no one I'd rather leading the trauma team,' she said quietly, and he frowned.

'You are *not* going to have an accident, but thank you for the compliment. But I have to learn to be less controlling with you, I can see that, and I will try.'

And he did.

Over the next few days he asked her opinion on everything and listened carefully, and Christy saw a whole new side to him.

Surely he couldn't be making this much effort just for the children, she thought to herself. Surely his behaviour was an indication that he still had feelings for her?

The only physical contact they'd had had been the passionate sex they'd shared the night of the Snow Ball. And that hadn't counted, she told herself miserably, because he'd been provoked.

Why was he still not touching her?

Alessandro had such a high sex drive that never

before in their marriage had she found herself in the position of having to initiate sex, but now she was starting to wonder whether she should go down that route.

But what if he rejected her?

She bit back a hysterical giggle as she prepared the children's lunch and got ready to take them to her mother's for an afternoon of Christmas shopping. It must be awful being a man, she decided. They faced rejection every time they went near a woman.

She was just pouring coffee into mugs when Alessandro strode into the room, talking into his phone.

She could tell from his responses that he was talking to Sean about a rescue, and when he snapped the phone shut she looked at him expectantly.

'Trouble?'

'A party of teenagers were climbing in the gully and it avalanched.'

Christy winced. She knew how dangerous that climb could be because she'd done it herself plenty of times when she'd been younger.

'How much do we know?'

Alessandro was already hauling equipment out of the utility room where it had been drying. 'Two of them were above it and managed to get to the top and raise the alarm. The third is stuck on a ledge.'

'So we'd do best to approach from the south-east ridge and then we'll be above him. It's just the *best* abseil,' Christy breathed, and Alessandro scowled at her.

'I always hated you doing that climb.'

She grinned. 'It was fun.'

'It was dangerous. And you have two children to think of now.'

Her smile faded. It was true, of course, and she would never take unnecessary risks. But at the same time she wished that sometimes he could think about *her*, rather than the children.

'So are we the advance party?'

Alessandro nodded. 'Yes, but it's going to take a large team to get him down if he's badly injured.'

Christy glanced out of the window. 'At least the weather looks pretty good. Should be able to fly a helicopter in this.'

Katy danced into the room. 'When are we going to Grandma's?'

'Right now.' Alessandro grabbed the rest of the equipment and strode out of the kitchen, with Christy and the children hurrying close behind.

They dropped the children and then Alessandro drove out of town towards the road that would allow them to take the fastest route to the gully.

The sun glistened on the snow and Christy frowned. 'Not a great day to climb that particular route,' she murmured, casting her mind back to her own experiences. 'The snow gets very soft if the sun is out.'

'They're fortunate that only one of them is injured,' Alessandro growled as he swung the car into the lay-by and switched off the engine. Jake and Sean walked towards them.

'We've got four hours before dark,' Sean said, his expression grim as he stared up the path they needed to take. 'Let's shift.'

They walked fast and reached the top of the gully within an hour and half.

Alessandro immediately abseiled down the

gully to assess the state of the injured boy, careful not to dislodge rocks as he went.

Below them, at the foot of the gully, Christy could see the deep, tumbled snow that had avalanched off the steep face.

'They were lucky,' she said to Jake, who was now beside her and delving into his pack for the ropes he was carrying. 'They could have been buried under that.'

She watched as Alessandro attached the boy to his rope and saw him reach for his radio. Then he spoke to Sean, passing on details of his injuries.

'We're going to need to lower him to the bottom of the gully on a stretcher.'

Jake rolled his eyes and Christy grinned.

It was the most equipment-intensive rescue that they performed and immediately she started to identify safe anchor points that could be used to secure ropes.

While Alessandro gave first aid to the casualty and tried to ward off hypothermia, Christy and Jake set up the lowering belay for the stretcher and handlers.

'This is going to be fun,' Jake muttered, as he

found another anchor point and then rigged the stretcher for a vertical lower. 'Which mad fools are going to volunteer to act as barrow boys?'

The stretcher would be held by a static rope at both ends and helped down by two 'barrow boys' who were responsible for abseiling down alongside the stretcher to control the descent.

Each rope was secured to the crag by five equalised anchor points, and by the time the team had finished preparing, ropes were criss-crossing the crag.

It took another hour of intensive teamwork to lower the casualty safely to the bottom and move him out of reach of further avalanches.

While all three teenagers were protected in a bivvy tent, Alessandro did a more detailed survey of the injured boy and Sean communicated with the helicopter.

Fifteen minutes later they heard the familiar clack-clack and the helicopter came up the valley towards them. The helicopter dropped an orange smoke bomb to give an indication of wind speed and direction and everyone made sure that everything was securely anchored down.

First Alessandro was winched into the helicopter, ready to receive the patient. Then the winch man was lifted with the stretcher across his waist, a high line preventing the stretcher from spinning round in the wind. Christy watched from the ground as the stretcher drew level with the open door and the winch operator helped ease the stretcher into the helicopter.

Then they jettisoned the high line and soared down the valley towards the hospital.

'Which leaves us to get ourselves off this hill in darkness and freezing cold,' Jake muttered. 'Why does Alessandro always manage to hitch a lift?'

'Because he's a brilliant A and E doctor,' Christy said as she started collecting equipment and preparing for their descent.

Jake looked at her. 'Hero-worship?'

She gave a wry smile as she pushed a rope into her rucksack. 'Possibly. But I think it's love, unfortunately.'

'Why unfortunately?'

'I don't know.' Christy heaved her pack onto her back. 'I suppose because I still don't really know where I stand with him.'

'Have you tried blunt conversation?'

She looked at him. 'I suppose I'm afraid to do that,' she said honestly. 'Afraid I might push him into saying something I don't want to hear.'

Like 'I don't really love you any more but I'm willing to make an effort because of the children'.

Jake glanced up at the lethal gully. 'You just went up there without batting an eyelid and now you're expecting me to believe that you're afraid of having a conversation with your husband?'

'That's me.' Christy scuffed at the snow with the toe of her boot. 'Miss Coward.'

'Hardly.' Jake waited as the team picked up the last of the equipment and then they all started their descent into the valley.

CHAPTER NINE

CHRISTY collected the children from her mother's and they were sparkly eyed, thoroughly over-excited and weighed down with various bags and rolls of wrapping paper.

'When Santa came down the chim*ney*,' Ben sang loudly, and Katy grimaced.

'*Don't* sing. I'll give you all my pocket money if you stop singing. It's gross. If Father Christmas hears you he'll take a detour because the noise is so terrible.'

Christy glanced in her rear view mirror. 'Did you guys buy anything with Grandma?'

'Loads,' Katy said happily, and Ben beamed.

'We bought you a—'

'Shut up!' Katy glared at him furiously. 'You don't tell people what their presents are, stupid.'

Christy sighed as she took the turning that led

to the barn. 'Don't say "shut up", Katy, it isn't nice, and don't call your brother stupid.'

'Well, having all your secrets blown by your baby brother isn't nice, and he is stupid,' Katy muttered. Christy parked the car and switched off the engine. She wondered what time Alessandro would be back. Hopefully not too late. She wanted to spend the evening with him. *And the night.*

Maybe it was time for her to take the initiative, she thought to herself as she undid her seat belt and turned off the headlights.

After all, she'd been the one to stalk away after their passionate encounter in the maze at the Snow Ball. She could hardly blame him for keeping his distance.

'Tomorrow is Christmas Eve,' Ben announced as he wriggled out of his seat belt and opened the car door. 'We can hang up our stockings. Do you think he's set off yet?'

'Who?' Christy dragged her mind back to the practicalities of life, rescued her wet gear from the boot and trudged towards the barn.

'Father Christmas, of course.' Ben frowned up at

her, his sweet face innocent and puzzled. 'I don't see how he can get round the whole world in one night, do you? If he doesn't set off until tomorrow, he's never going to make it. You say there's no such thing as magic, so what will he do?'

'I…er…' Christy struggled for a suitable reply as she found her keys and opened the front door. 'Well, we can't understand everything that happens in the world,' she hedged, 'and I think Father Christmas leaves the exact amount of time he needs to do his job,' she said finally. Katy rolled her eyes.

'He won't need long for you, anyway,' she told her brother loftily. 'You haven't been that good this year.'

Ben's face crumpled. 'That's *not* true.'

'You've both been good,' said Christy, keen to hurry them inside and avoid a row. 'Who fancies some mince pies? I made them earlier.'

'Me!' both children shrieked simultaneously and they piled into the kitchen, dropping bags, hats and gloves onto the table and dragging chairs across the floor.

'Grandma was telling us about her nativity

play,' Katy said, biting into a mince pie. 'Mary had nits and the two halves of the donkey started fighting halfway through.'

Christy smiled as she reached into the cupboard for a large casserole pot. 'Your grandma always has good stories at Christmas.'

Her mother taught the reception class at the local primary school and the highlight of the year was the nativity play.

'Then the innkeeper said, "We're totally empty, how many rooms would you like?"' Katy continued, curling her leg under her as she helped herself to another mince pie. 'And Joseph and Mary were so confused they completely forgot their lines and then one of the shepherds tripped and fell on the baby Jesus and—listen to this because it's the best one—one of the three kings said, "I bring Frankenstein."'

Christy laughed and Ben frowned. 'What's wrong with that?'

'Because the King brings frankincense. Franken*stein* was a monster.' Katy yawned. 'A bit like you, really.' She reached an arm across the table and Christy removed the plate quickly.

'Enough, or you'll be too full to eat your tea. Go and play a game while I get supper ready.'

'Let's play squash the present.' Katy slipped off the chair and grabbed Ben's hand. 'We'll squeeze and prod and shake and see if we can guess what's in the parcels. Then we'll see if we're right on Christmas Day.'

'If you haven't broken it,' Christy pointed out dryly, dropping onion into melted butter and frying it gently. She was wondering if she had time to take a shower before Alessandro arrived home.

Quickly she browned meat, added stock, wine and herbs and slid the casserole dish into the oven.

The children were sprawled on the living-room rug, bickering over a game of Monopoly that they'd started the day before.

Christy smiled as she watched them. They argued but there was no denying the love between them. Her children were gorgeous, she thought to herself.

Deciding that she could safely take a shower without war breaking out, she sped upstairs, stripped off quickly and padded into the bathroom.

She showered quickly, washed her hair and then padded into the bedroom and stared into her wardrobe, hoping for inspiration.

What was she going to wear? Something that would ensure that Alessandro would notice her.

But nothing too obvious or she'd look ridiculous.

Katy wandered into the room, wearing jeans, a baggy jumper and stripy socks. 'Are you going to dress up for Dad?'

Christy felt the colour rush into her cheeks. 'Why do you say that?'

'Because you've got a funny look on your face and you're staring into your wardrobe instead of grabbing a pair of jeans.'

Was that what she usually did? Christy frowned. She wore a uniform for work and it was true that when she arrived home she often just pulled on the nearest thing, which was invariably jeans and a jumper.

'Wear red,' Katy advised, springing onto the bed and sitting cross-legged. 'Dad always looks at you in a funny way when you wear red.'

Wondering just when her daughter had become so observant, Christy reached into her wardrobe and pulled out the red dress. It was made of the softest jersey fabric and skimmed over her curves. She'd always loved it but she hardly had occasion to wear it any more.

She'd been wearing it the night of their anniversary. The night he hadn't turned up. The night she'd decided to leave in order to shake him up.

What exactly was happening to their relationship now?

Certainly things between them had improved dramatically. They were working together and in many ways their relationship felt the way it had before they'd had children.

But did he really care for her or was he making an effort because he valued the institution of the family so much?

She wriggled into the dress, slipped her feet into a pair of high-heeled shoes that she loved and frowned at her hair.

Should she try and straighten it?

It tumbled in crazy, dizzying waves down her back, gold and russet mingling with rich copper. Occasionally she had it blow-dried straight, but left to its own devices it curled and twisted.

Wild, passionate hair, Alessandro had always called it.

Remembering his preference, she left the straighteners in her drawer.

'Mum?' Katy slid off the bed and hesitated, suddenly looking less confident than usual. 'Are we going back to London after Christmas?'

Christy froze. Were they? She honestly didn't know. She wanted Alessandro to ask her to stay. She wanted him to give her some indication that he wanted her. Yes, he was angry that she'd left and taken the children, but that wasn't the same as missing her, was it?

'I don't know,' she said quietly, knowing that Katy was old enough to deserve at least part of the truth. 'I don't know, sweetheart, but we're trying to work everything out.'

Katy chewed her lip. 'If I could only have one thing this Christmas, it would be you and Dad back together and living here like we always did.'

Christy felt her stomach turn. She'd stay, she told herself. Whatever happened, she'd stay for the sake of the children. How could she do anything else? Her own needs really didn't matter, she told herself as she fixed a reassuring smile on her face and pulled her daughter into her arms.

'You don't have to worry,' she whispered soothingly. 'Everything is going to be fine for you.'

But would it be fine for her?

Only time could tell.

The casserole was cooked and she was mashing potatoes when she finally heard Alessandro's key in the door.

'Daddy!' The children hurtled towards him and he lifted them both into a hug.

Watching from the kitchen door, Christy felt her heart turn over. Whatever happened, she wouldn't be leaving, she told herself. She couldn't deprive the children of their right to live with their father. But where did that leave her?

He lifted Ben into his arms, swung him round and then laid him on the rug and tickled him mercilessly while Christy laughed.

'You're getting him all wound up,' she scolded, 'and just before bedtime.'

'Isn't that what fathers are supposed to do?' He straightened in a lithe, athletic movement and looked at her properly for the first time. His gaze slid slowly down her slender frame and then his eyes returned to hers.

'I'm very tired,' he drawled in a soft voice, stepping over Ben and walking towards her. 'I was thinking of an early night. Does that suit you?'

There was a wicked gleam in his eyes that made her heart miss a beat. 'I'm pretty tired, too,' she croaked, and Katy cleared her throat.

'Well, before you both fall asleep, could you possibly feed us? We're both starving.'

Christy dragged her eyes away from Alessandro's burning gaze. 'Oh, yes—dinner's ready.' Suddenly flustered, aware of his eyes on her, she hurried back into the kitchen and lifted the warmed plates from the oven. 'Come on, then. Sit up.'

Suddenly she just wanted dinner to be over.

She wanted to be with Alessandro.

'Daddy, will you read me a story?'

'Of course.' Alessandro smiled at Katy and then glanced at Christy. 'Is that OK with you? Do you need help clearing up the kitchen?'

He hoped she'd say no. Clearing up the kitchen was his least favourite task and perhaps she knew that because she gave a smile and shook her head.

'You go and read to the children. I'll finish off here and meet you upstairs.'

Suddenly in the grip of a serious attack of lust, Alessandro had to force himself to follow his daughter into her pink, girly bedroom.

'Just a quick story tonight,' he muttered, as he scanned her bookshelves for something that had few pages. He wanted to be with Katy's mother.

Katy reached for a huge fat book. 'I'm reading this, but you don't have to finish it so you can relax.'

Alessandro stared at the book and decided that if it fell on someone's foot, he'd be taking them to the operating theatre. 'Well, that's a relief.'

Katy snuggled into bed. 'Have you bought Mum something for Christmas?'

Disturbed from his contemplation of how little he could get away with, Alessandro looked up. 'Of course.'

'Well, what is it?'

Alessandro frowned. 'It's a surprise. I can't—'

'Dad.' Katy sat up and wrapped her arms round her knees. 'You need to tell me what it is. Presents are important to women.'

'Which is why I chose your mother something that I know she's going to love,' Alessandro said smugly, thinking of the box in his boot.

'So?' Katy looked at him expectantly, and Alessandro sighed.

'All right, I'll tell you but you're not to tell your mother.'

Katy rolled her eyes. 'I'm eleven, Dad. I know about secrets. It's Ben that's the blabbermouth around here, not me.'

Alessandro smiled. 'All right—I've bought her a food processor.'

Katy stared at him in shocked silence. 'You bought her *what*?'

'A food processor.' Alessandro shrugged. 'You know—she uses it all the time and hers broke and—'

'I know what a food processor is,' Katy hissed, glancing towards the door to check that no one was listening, 'but, Dad, that *isn't a good present*.'

'I bought the most expensive model in the shop.'

Katy shook her head frantically. 'You have to get her something else, something that girls like.'

Wondering how he came to be sitting on a pink bedcover, taking advice from his eleven-year-old daughter, Alessandro lifted an eyebrow. 'Such as?'

'Something more personal. Jewellery.'

'I've never bought your mother jewellery. She doesn't wear jewellery.'

'Well, she can't wear what you've never bought her,' Katy pointed out logically, and Alessandro gritted his teeth.

'It's a waste of money.'

'Dad, you're totally loaded,' Katy said scornfully. 'What's the point of having money if you don't spend it?'

'She doesn't like jewellery.'

'All right.' Katy lay back on the pillow with a weary look on her face. 'Give her the food processor and let's see what happens.'

Alessandro hesitated and then leaned forward to kiss her. 'Don't worry,' he said softly, 'everything is going to turn out fine.'

'Not if you give her a blender, it isn't,' Katy muttered, rolling onto her side and yanking the duvet up over her shoulders. 'Our Christmas is going to be well and truly puréed. You might want to think about that before you wrap it up. When I grow up I'm going to write a book called *The Inner Workings of a Woman's Mind*, and you're going to be my first customer.'

It was a novelty, Alessandro mused as he strolled along to the master bedroom suite, to be told by his eleven-year-old daughter that he didn't understand women.

Should he be amused or insulted?

Christy didn't care about things that glittered, he told himself as he swiftly undressed and strolled towards the shower.

She cared about the things that mattered, like their relationship and the children. *Por Dios—* he hit the buttons on the shower and closed his eyes as hot water streamed over his body—he'd married her so quickly that they hadn't even bothered with an engagement.

And he spent money on the things that mattered. She had a beautiful house, a reliable car…

By the time he'd wrapped a towel round his waist and walked back into the bedroom, he'd convinced himself that he'd shown his love in any number of ways that truly mattered.

And then he saw Christy standing by the bed, lost in thought as she twisted the wedding band on her finger.

What was she thinking? he wondered.

Suddenly his stomach gave a lurch. Was she thinking of taking it off? They still hadn't had a conversation about their future and he was afraid to bring the subject up in case he precipitated the unthinkable.

Christy returning to London.

'I bought you that ring in a tiny shop in the East End of London where we were working,' he said quietly, and she glanced up quickly and smiled.

'That's right. We were in such a hurry, weren't we?'

He studied her face for a long moment. Tried to read her mind. 'Too much of a hurry, *querida*?'

For a moment she didn't answer and then she gave a tiny shrug. 'Maybe. We were young. We didn't really think things through.'

Was she implying that, had she had time to think things through, she wouldn't have married him?

Driven by an intense need to protect what was his and prove his love, Alessandro moved towards her and saw her eyes narrow and darken.

He recognised the look.

She wanted him as much as he wanted her.

With a rough oath, he crossed the room and brought his mouth down on hers in a fierce kiss, forgetting that he'd vowed to give her space. He didn't want to give her space. She was his. And he wanted her.

Now.

And she wanted him. He could tell from the way she responded to his kiss.

She was as hungry and desperate as he was.

With a tiny murmur she slid her hands down his back and he felt her fingers jerk on the towel that he'd hooked around his waist.

His mouth still on hers, he undressed her swiftly and then lifted her and lowered her onto the centre of the bed.

She was all silken flesh and warm woman, the subtle scent of her perfume casting a sensual spell that threatened his ability to operate on any level other than the most basic.

With a groan of pure, masculine possession, he covered her body with his, feeling soft curves meet hard muscle and relishing the differences between them. She looked delicate but he knew her to be strong and passionate. Knew that he wouldn't hurt her. That she was as eager as he was.

His mouth feasted on hers and his hand slid down to the top of her thighs and lingered.

He trapped her sob with his mouth, felt her body writhe under his and used his fingers to touch her intimately.

Reminding himself that he'd planned to make love to her slowly, Alessandro tried to pull away and gain some semblance of control over his reactions, but she wrapped one leg over his and drew it upwards, urging him towards her.

Wondering why he suddenly had the restraint of a teenager, Alessandro slid a hand under her hips, lifted her and thrust deep. He felt her fingers dig hard into his waist, and he thrust again, muffling her sob with his kiss.

'*Por Dios*, you feel incredible,' he said hoarsely, lifting his mouth just enough to enable him to see her face. Her cheeks were flushed, her eyes were bright and fevered and her mouth was bruised from the pressure of his. And she'd never looked more beautiful.

He shifted his position and moved, knowing exactly how to drive her upwards towards the ultimate pleasure. Her eyes drifted shut and he slid a hand into her soft, silken hair.

'Look at me, *querida*.' He gave a soft groan and brought his mouth down on hers again. *Never had he had to work so hard to find the control he needed.* 'I want you to look at me.'

He didn't know why it suddenly felt so important but it was, and perhaps she felt it too because her eyes opened and stared into his. And he saw everything there. Love. Passion.

Her fingers curled into his back and he saw her cheeks flush and her breath quicken and knew that she was close, but he held back, refusing to allow her the release she craved until he was ready.

So he slowed the rhythm and she groaned in protest and tried to shift her hips, tried to force the pace.

'Alessandro.' Her voice was a breathless whisper of desperation. 'Please, oh, please…'

Deciding that they had the whole night ahead of them so control didn't really matter that much, Alessandro drove deeper inside her and felt the sudden clench of lust as she gripped him.

And then he felt her body tighten around his and he ceased to think altogether as they reached the peak together in one long shower of erotic sensation that left them both breathless and unable to speak.

Christy lay with her eyes closed, feeling blissfully happy and content for the first time in months.

Alessandro loved her.

She knew he loved her.

The night hadn't been about the children or staying together for the family. It had been about them as a couple. About expressing their love.

He still hadn't told her that he wasn't going to let her leave, but he would. She knew he would.

He was probably just being sensitive about bringing the subject up.

Tomorrow he'd tell her that she was staying

in that arrogant, autocratic manner of his. She'd say yes.

And Christmas would be perfect.

Christy was making breakfast when the phone rang.

Before she could answer it, Alessandro strolled into the kitchen and picked up the handset. His eyes lingered on her flushed cheeks for a moment and then he gave a slow smile of masculine satisfaction and she blushed deeply.

Help, she thought as she turned back to the hob to stir the porridge. She was behaving like a teenager.

She was so lost in her own dreamy thoughts that she didn't even listen to Alessandro's conversation—didn't even register that he was off the phone until he walked across the kitchen and poured himself a large mug of coffee.

'That was your brother,' he said, and his voice was so cold that she looked at him in alarm.

'Is everything all right? Has something happened?' A moment ago Alessandro had been looking at her as if he had every intention of skipping work and taking her back to bed. Now he looked remote and unapproachable and nothing like the man who'd made love to her all night.

'Nothing's wrong,' he said smoothly, 'except that his other practice nurse has slipped on the ice and broken her wrist. So he wonders if you'd consider coming back immediately after Christmas.'

Her heart flipped. Surely this was the moment when he was going to tell her that she had to stay, *that he wasn't going to let her leave.*

'Well, I hadn't thought about going that quickly…' She hesitated, waited for him to interrupt her and tell her that she wasn't going at all, but he stood still, studying her face with brooding intensity.

What was he thinking?

'I'll ring Peter back,' she said quickly, 'and chat about it.'

'Fine.' His mouth set in a grim line, Alessandro slammed his mug down on the table so hard that most of the liquid sloshed over the wood. Then he strode from the room, narrowly avoiding a collision with Katy, who was on her way to find breakfast.

She watched her father go with a look of surprise and then saw the pool of liquid on the table. 'Now I know where Ben gets it from,' she said wearily as she walked round the table and reached for a cloth. 'Spilling drinks is obviously a genetic defect. Remind me to screen any man I marry—I don't want to spend my life mopping up puddles.'

Christy was too miserable even to raise a smile. Now what?

She thought back to the conversation they'd had when he'd walked out of the shower the night before. He'd been talking about the time they'd met. Hadn't he implied last night that they'd married in too much of a hurry?

Obviously he was the one who was regretting their whirlwind courtship.

Perhaps, after all, he wanted to be free to date women like Katya but was much too traditional to make that decision himself.

So he was expecting her to make it.

Why hadn't he told her that she couldn't

leave? She felt tears prick her eyes as she turned off the heat and poured porridge into bowls for the children.

'Mum, this isn't the story of Goldilocks, you know.' Katy stared at the meagre contents of her bowl. 'And I'm not baby bear. That's never going to keep me warm on a cold day.'

Realising that she'd only put a spoonful in the bowl, Christy gave a wan smile and filled the bowl to the top.

'Are you all right, Mum?'

No, Christy thought, suppressing a hysterical giggle. She was far from all right.

It appeared that her marriage was well and truly over and that wasn't what she wanted. It wasn't what she'd ever wanted.

Everything had gone utterly, miserably wrong and it was mostly her fault for leaving in the first place.

It didn't matter that she'd intended him to follow her the same day and make up.

All that mattered was that she adored him and that he didn't seem to want her with him any more.

And every time she tried to remind herself that

last night he'd been loving and caring, that over the past days he'd listened to her and treated her like a woman, nothing changed the fact that he hadn't told her that she couldn't leave.

And Alessandro had never, *ever* had problems saying what he wanted.

So if he hadn't asked her then there was only one possible explanation.

He was hoping that she'd go back to London.

CHAPTER TEN

SHE spent Christmas Eve with the children and they went for a walk in the forest, stamping footprints into virgin snow and piercing the muffled silence with their excited squeals.

After the inevitable snowball fight, they returned to the barn wet and happy and Christy set about drying clothes and making dinner.

Would this be the last time she did this?

Would this be their last ever Christmas as a family?

She stood for a moment and looked around the kitchen, the kitchen she'd chosen so carefully. Three more days. In three more days she'd be leaving this and she'd probably never cook in this room again.

Tears stung her eyes.

'Mum, I want to leave a chocolate roll for

Santa.' Ben was beside her, his eyes huge and shining, a pair of furry brown antlers jammed onto his head. 'Everyone leaves mince pies and he must be really bored with it, don't you think? I mean mince pies are great, but if you think of the population of the world, that's a lot of pastry, isn't it?'

Blinking back the tears, Christy smiled and reached into the cupboard for a little chocolate roll. 'Good idea,' she said huskily. 'Leave him this with a little note. I'm sure he'll be really pleased.'

'And carrots for the reindeer.' Ben squinted up at her, the bells on his antlers jangling. 'Why are you crying?'

'Me? Crying? Never.' Her smile widened and she wondered if her face would crack with the effort. 'I've been chopping onions for tea.'

'I hate onions.'

'They're for Daddy's tea,' Christy said quickly, turning her back on him and washing her hands. 'Go and put that cake out now, before you forget.'

'I can't wait for Daddy to come home so we can hang up our stockings like we always do.'

Family tradition. Routine.

Thinking of Ben's innocent face, Christy thought her heart might break.

Why did life have to go so very wrong? Wasn't there something she could have done to have fixed it?

Was this all her fault?

Katy wandered into the room. 'I love Christmas Eve even more than I love Christmas.'

Pulling herself together, Christy turned round, the smile still in place. 'Why's that?'

'Because you have all the excitement and anticipation. It's all still to come.' Katy danced round the kitchen, her ponytail swinging. 'And Christmas Eve feels so Christmassy. More Christmassy than Christmas Day. Tomorrow's going to be brilliant, isn't it, Mum?'

'Yes.'

Katy stopped dancing and looked at her. 'Everything's going to be OK, Mum.'

How did you explain to an eleven-year-old girl who still thought that life was perfect that everything was going to be anything but OK?

Keeping up a brave front was proving exhausting and she was almost relieved when Alessandro arrived home. At least the children might stop noticing her.

They ate dinner as a family and Christy was glad of the excited chatter of the children. It meant that she didn't have to speak, which was a relief because she honestly didn't know what to say with Alessandro looking so icily remote across the table.

Not only did he not want her to stay but, judging from the look on his face, he couldn't wait for Christmas to be over so that she would leave.

After dinner, she watched with a lump in her throat as Alessandro helped Ben fasten his huge red sock to the fireplace and write his letter to Father Christmas.

Finally the children were tucked up in bed and the house was silent.

When she was sure that the children were asleep, Christy tiptoed back downstairs and stuffed the stockings. It was a ritual that she and Alessandro normally performed together with the help of chilled champagne and smoked salmon. Memories filled her brain. *How many years had they ended the evening by making love on the huge rug in front of the fire?*

But not tonight.

Tonight, Christmas Eve had lost its magic.

She went to bed, but her mind was too full of thoughts to allow her to sleep, so eventually she padded back downstairs to the living room. Staring out of the huge windows into the darkness, she watched the soft swirl of snowflakes.

'Aren't you coming to bed?' Alessandro's voice came from directly behind her and she tensed, afraid to turn in case she gave herself away.

'Don't you ever wish you were still small and believed in Father Christmas?' she breathed softly, watching the snow hit the pane and slide downwards leaving a watery trail. 'It's one of the most magical things about childhood. Believing in the impossible.'

'So what would you want him to bring you?'

She was silent for a moment. 'Love,' she said softly, without turning to look at him. 'It's the only thing that really matters in the end. Everything else is nothing without love.'

He didn't answer and the still silence of the

room seemed to close them in and wrap itself around them.

'Then I hope you find it,' he said hoarsely, and she heard the firm tread of his step as he turned and walked away, leaving her with only her sadness for company.

'Mummy, can we get up now?' Ben's excited voice was the first thing she heard when she finally woke the following morning after about two hours' sleep.

'He's been prising my eyelids open for the past three hours,' Katy complained as she bounced onto her parents' bed. 'He keeps saying, "Is it time yet?" like a parrot.'

'That phrase is probably first cousin to "Are we there yet?"' Alessandro muttered, sitting up in bed and stifling a yawn.

Christy risked a glance at him and saw that he looked exhausted, too.

And tense.

Was being with her really that much of a strain?

Oh, for crying out loud. It was Christmas Day and nothing, not even her crumbling, disintegrating marriage, was going to spoil it!

'Come on, then.' Pushing away the heavy bands of stress and tiredness that threatened to crush her skull, she slid out of bed and pulled on her silk robe.

The children careered downstairs, shrieking with excitement, and she followed more slowly, watching their pleasure with an indulgent smile.

'He's been, *he's been*,' Ben shouted, dancing up to his stocking and lifting it. 'And look—he's eaten the chocolate roll and left a footprint.'

Sure enough, a large, dusty footprint lay in front of the fireplace and Christy gave a smile. Alessandro must have come back downstairs during the night to make that, she thought to herself. He'd always done it, even when the children had been too young to notice. *He was a brilliant father.*

He walked into the room moments later, his dark eyes heavy with sleep, his jeans half-undone and his T-shirt rumpled. He'd obviously reached for the first thing in his wardrobe and still he managed to look impossibly sexy, she thought with something close to exasperation.

Why couldn't she look at him and feel nothing? How did you stifle a love as powerful as hers? *How did you carry on with life?*

'Has Father Christmas been coming down my chimney without wiping his feet again?' Alessandro glowered at the footprint and Ben giggled.

'Do you think he brought the reindeer?'

Alessandro raised an eyebrow. 'Into my living room? I hope not.'

'Come on, Ben.' Determined not to dwell on Alessandro, she turned back to the children. 'What has he brought you?'

Christmas Day had begun. They opened the presents in their stockings, ate breakfast together and then went to the carol service at the local church.

Wrapped up warmly in a long coat, Christy listened to the pure voices of the choirboys and felt a lump in her throat.

It was normally her favourite part of Christmas but today it just seemed to make her feel even sadder.

'Hey.' A masculine voice came from behind

her. 'I hope my lunch isn't burning while you're here.'

It was Jake.

Having him for the day would be a welcome distraction, she thought to herself as she turned to acknowledge his presence with a quick smile.

'Come on, Mum.' Katy grabbed her hand as they arrived back at the barn to the delicious smells of turkey. 'Time for all the other presents now.'

Her parents arrived moments later and suddenly the house took on the chaotic, crazy feel that only ever happened at Christmas.

'I have to go and spend some time in the kitchen,' Christy began, but Katy shook her head.

'It can wait. It doesn't matter if lunch is late. We can always eat crisps to keep us going.'

'You cannot eat crisps!'

Katy grinned. 'Just winding you up, Mum.'

Christy gave a weak smile and followed her daughter through to the living room.

Jake and Alessandro were talking by the fireplace and Katy dropped to her knees and dragged the presents out from under the tree.

'This one is for Daddy, from Grandma…'

Christy watched as everyone opened presents and tried not to mind that Alessandro didn't seem to have bought her anything.

Why would he? She was only here under sufferance. Because he wanted Christmas with his children, and she came as part of the package.

Eventually the pressure grew too much and she retired to the kitchen.

It was all right, she told herself firmly as she checked the roast potatoes and stirred the cranberry sauce. She'd cope. Whatever happened, she'd cope.

She was concentrating so hard on not breaking down that she didn't hear the kitchen door open and close. She wasn't aware of another person in the room until she heard Alessandro's deep, dark drawl from directly behind her.

'There are things that I have to say,' he said tightly, 'and you're not going to like them. But I'm going to say them anyway.'

Oh, dear God, not now, she thought. She had to produce Christmas dinner for seven people and she couldn't do that if he'd just told her that he didn't love her any more and that he wanted her to go back to London. Knowing that it was the truth was quite different from hearing it.

'We can talk later, Alessandro,' she said quickly, sticking her face in the oven to check the turkey and resisting the temptation to leave it there. 'This probably isn't the best time.'

'I don't care about that. You have to listen.' He strode across the kitchen and pulled her away from the oven. Strong hands closed over her shoulders, forcing her to look at him.

'All right, then.' She said the words with weary resignation. 'This is about me going back to London, isn't it? It's fine, Alessandro. I'll leave the day after tomorrow.'

'You're not going anywhere.' His voice was a threatening growl and then he cursed softly and released her, taking a step backwards. 'I'm doing this all wrong but— I've got you a present—let's start with that.'

He seemed to be fumbling for words and she considered it a point in his favour that he appeared to have lost his usually fluent English.

Obviously he wasn't finding it easy and perversely she was glad about that. She didn't want him to find it easy.

'A present?' She stared at him with a lack of comprehension. Given the gravity of their conversation, mention of a Christmas present suddenly jarred. Material gifts were so unimportant, she thought dully, but she forced herself to smile and look interested. 'For me?'

'Of course, for you.'

He would have bought her something because of the children, she reasoned. Because Katy would have asked questions if there'd been nothing for her. 'Why didn't you give it to me when we were all round the tree?'

'Because this is a special gift from me to you and I don't want to share it.'

Not because of the children, then.

What sort of special gift was he buying her? she wondered with wry humour. A one-way train ticket south? Frosted divorce papers?

He reached into his pocket and withdrew a small box wrapped in glittering paper.

'Oh, it's pretty…' And so unlike Alessandro,

she thought as she took the box, feeling the sudden uneven thump of her heart. *Don't be ridiculous, Christy*, she told herself firmly. *This can't be anything special. It can't be.*

'Open it,' he urged in a husky voice. 'Open it, *querida*.'

A lump sprang into her throat. Why was he calling her darling when they were two days away from ending their marriage for ever?

Wanting to get the moment over as quickly as possible, she ripped off the paper and saw a small velvet box.

Jewellery.

It had to be jewellery.

Suddenly she wanted to laugh and cry at the same time. She'd spent twelve Christmases with Alessandro and he'd never bought her jewellery and he decided to do it on their last one.

Why?

Trying to find the answer to that question, she looked up at him and saw an unusual degree of tension in his handsome face.

'Aren't you going to look?' His voice bordered on the impatient and he stretched out a lean, bronzed hand and flipped the box open. 'Do you like it?'

He sounded nervous and she'd never known Alessandro to be nervous of anything before. He never questioned himself but tackled life with an enviable degree of self-confidence. But today that confidence appeared to be lacking.

She glanced down at the box in her hand and felt the floor shift. Nestled in a bed of rich, deep blue silk lay a huge, sparkling diamond. It twinkled and sparkled under the kitchen lights and she stared at it stupidly.

Finally she found her voice. 'What is it?'

'It's the ring I should have given you twelve years ago,' Alessandro said gruffly. 'But I'm giving it to you now. If you'll wear it.'

'But—'

'I'm not great at speeches, so let me just say what I have to say.' He jabbed long fingers through his glossy hair and took a deep breath. 'I fell in love with you the day I saw you. Impossible, I know, but that's how it was. You were so beautiful, so warm and kind and yet so fiery and passionate. I'd never met a woman like you before and after I saw you I never looked again. And I've never stopped loving you. And if you love someone you're supposed to be able to set them free—let them go. I told myself that I'd let you go if that was what you wanted—'

'Alessandro—'

'I promised not to order or command so I can't force you to stay,' Alessandro said hoarsely, 'but I'm willing to beg. Will you stay, Christy? Will you stay if I beg?'

Beg?

She stared at him. None of it made sense. 'But you don't love me—'

'*How* can you say that?' He stared at her a look of stunned incredulity in his dark eyes. 'When have I ever led you to believe that I don't love you?'

She chewed her lip. 'Loads of reasons,' she said finally. 'You didn't follow me to London, you put me in the spare room and we've been lying in the same bed and you haven't made love to me—'

'Because when I *did* make love to you,' he exploded, the natural volatility of his Mediterranean temperament bubbling to the surface, 'you slapped me!'

'It was sex.'

'It was *love, querida*,' he said hoarsely, and she shook her head slowly.

'You never once said you loved me.'

'I did.'

'No,' she said patiently. 'You didn't.'

'So…' He spread his hands in a supremely Latin gesture. 'I had other things on my mind at the time, like the fact that you looked so incredibly sexy and we hadn't been together for weeks and—' He broke off and gave an apologetic smile. 'And I am a man and verbal communication isn't my forte. I'm working on it.'

'I thought you'd stopped loving me.'

He stared at her in shocked silence. 'I've never stopped loving you.'

Hope flared and she squashed it down ruthlessly. 'You've never stopped loving me?'

'Of course not. I know I'm not perfect.' He frowned slightly as he said the words, as if admitting such a fact was difficult, 'and I realise that I've done many things wrong. Seeing you in A and E and in the mountain rescue team made me realise how many skills you have that you're not using. You have made so many sacrifices for the family.'

'They weren't sacrifices,' Christy murmured, but he shook his head.

'You made this family work. You made it possible for me to live the life I wanted to lead. And I neglected you as a woman. I can see that now.'

She sucked in a breath. 'Alessandro—'

'You have to let me finish,' he breathed, taking the box and removing the ring. 'Over the past two weeks I have tried so hard not to be controlling and bossy and I promise to work on that but even so, I can't let you leave again. I know I drive you crazy but you love me, Christy. Over the last two weeks I've become more and more sure about that.'

She swallowed hard. 'Of course I love you. And I didn't mean to leave—at least, not in the way that you mean. You weren't listening to me and I thought it was the only way to get through to you. I thought you'd come after me—'

'You didn't mean to leave? What do you mean, you didn't mean to leave?'

'It was only ever supposed to be for the weekend,' she confessed, pushing aside the last

vestiges of her pride in an effort to save their relationship. 'I thought you'd come after me and
drag me back.'

He ran a hand over his roughened jaw. 'Am I
really that controlling?'

'Yes. But not on that occasion, obviously.
Ironic, really. The one time I wanted you to come
and drag me back, you didn't do it.'

'It seems that I'm not the only one who is
hopeless at communicating. When I realised
you'd left I was totally and utterly devastated,'
he groaned, sliding a hand into her hair and
tilting her head so that he could look into her
eyes. 'I thought you didn't love me any more and
I could hardly blame you, because I missed our
anniversary—'

'It wasn't about our anniversary,' she interrupted him in a soft voice, needing to explain.
'We just didn't feel like a couple any more.'

'I suppose I was suffering from that old cliché
of taking you for granted.' He gave a shrug and
a self-deprecating smile. 'I came home and you
were always here. And then one day you weren't
and I had the shock of my life.'

'So why didn't you come after me?'

'I genuinely didn't realise that was what you wanted, although I should have done, of course. I've lived with you long enough to understand your temper.' His voice was soft and he dragged his thumb over her cheek in a gentle caress. 'For once in my life I was trying to think of you. I wanted you back but you were obviously so fed up with me that I thought you needed time and space so I left you alone.'

'And I thought you didn't want me.'

'Then you arrived back here looking stunningly gorgeous and promptly slept in the spare room.'

'You *put* me in the spare room,' she reminded him, and he gave a wry smile,

'Another major error of judgement on my part. I was expecting you to refuse to sleep there. *Always* you sleep in my bed.'

He sounded so much like the old Alessandro that she gave a soft smile. 'Thank goodness we had some help from the children or I'd still be in there,'

'*Sí*—because we are both so stubborn and hot-tempered, *gatita*.' He gave a groan and lowered his mouth to hers, dropping a lingering kiss on her mouth. 'Perhaps if I was a cool Englishman, none of this would have happened.'

'If you were a cool Englishman,' she muttered against his mouth, 'I never would have married you.'

He lifted his head a fraction. 'Is that true? I'm always very aware that I didn't give you a chance to date other men and I confess I was worried about Jake.'

'Jake has only ever been the very best friend to both of us. And I didn't want to date other men. But what about you?' She forced herself to ask the question she'd dreaded asking. 'I was worried about Katya. I thought you might be interested in her…' She left the statement hanging and his eyes narrowed, one ebony brow lifted in question.

'Have I *ever* given you reason not to trust me?'

'No.' She shook her head. 'But our marriage was on the rocks and—'

He placed his fingers over his lips. 'Don't say it,' he breathed, 'because it isn't the truth and it never was. We are both stormy, passionate people and our journey through life is never going to be in calm waters.'

'I thought you only wanted me to stay because of the children.' Dizzy from his kiss and the hard press of his body against hers, she stared up at him and he shook his head.

'Never,' he said hoarsely, reaching for her hand and sliding the ring on her finger. 'I married you in haste and I've loved you deeply ever since. I wanted you to stay because I love you and I can't live without you. And this is the engagement ring I should have given you twelve years ago.'

Her heart thumped hard against her chest as she stared at the ring in delighted fascination. It shone and sparkled on her finger. 'I've never seen anything more beautiful in my life,' she murmured, 'but I still don't understand one thing…'

His mouth was close to hers. 'What's that?'

'If you love me and you want me to stay, why didn't you say so when Pete rang, asking me to go back early?'

'Because you'd accused me of being controlling! I was giving you a choice, *querida*.' He gave a wry smile. 'But you weren't making the choice I wanted you to make. I assumed you'd only come home because of the children and with Christmas over you had no reason to stay.'

'And I thought you didn't want me. Alessandro, I came home for Christmas for me, not for the children. The children just gave me the excuse I'd been looking for.'

'And you say we kids are complicated.' A voice came from the doorway behind them, and they both turned.

Katy was standing in the doorway, arms folded and tinsel in her hair. Her eyes were on the ring that Christy was wearing. 'Nice present, Dad,' she said softly, and Alessandro gave her a slow smile, his arms still around his wife.

'I'm glad you think so,' he drawled, and Katy smiled.

'So, are we finally a happy family?'

Jake strolled into the kitchen and looped an arm round his goddaughter's shoulders. 'You shouldn't be watching this, angel. It's probably age restricted.'

Katy rolled her eyes. 'I'm almost twelve. I

know *everything*. The next thing is they'll probably go and mate or something. Pretty gross at their age, but there you are.'

Alessandro stared in stunned amazement, Christy blushed and Jake threw back his head and laughed. 'Well, my friends?' He stared at them quizzically. 'Have you sorted things out?'

Ben dashed into the kitchen with an armful of toys. 'Grandma says, is there a cloth? I spilled my drink.'

'Oh, what's new?' Katy gave a long-suffering sigh. 'Father Christmas should have stuck a jumbo box of kitchen roll in your stocking. Don't worry, Mum. You stay talking to Dad. I'll sort it out.' She hustled her brother out of the room and Jake watched them go, a smile playing around his firm mouth.

'She's growing up,' he said quietly, and Alessandro frowned.

'Don't say that. I'm not prepared for hormones or boyfriends.'

Jake rubbed his jaw, his blue eyes bright with humour. 'I'd say you're pretty good at defending what's yours.' The smile faded and he looked at both of them. 'You two were meant to be together. Always. Remember that.'

And with that he turned and left the room, closing the door quietly behind him.

Christy turned to Alessandro. 'The turkey is cooked and the roast potatoes are on the point of burning. We ought to serve dinner.'

He gave her a wicked smile. 'When are we going to mate?'

'Later.' She couldn't remember ever feeling so happy and she flung her arms round him and held him tight. 'Oh, Alessandro, this is the best present. All I wanted was for you to love me. For us to be a family.'

'And all I wanted was you, *querida*.' His voice was husky as he lifted her hand to his lips and kissed it, his eyes holding hers. 'Always. Merry Christmas.'

MEDICAL ROMANCE™

Large Print

Titles for the next six months…

June

THE MIDWIFE'S CHRISTMAS MIRACLE Sarah Morgan
ONE NIGHT TO WED Alison Roberts
A VERY SPECIAL PROPOSAL Josie Metcalfe
THE SURGEON'S MEANT-TO-BE BRIDE Amy Andrews
A FATHER BY CHRISTMAS Meredith Webber
A MOTHER FOR HIS BABY Leah Martyn

July

THE SURGEON'S MIRACLE BABY Carol Marinelli
A CONSULTANT CLAIMS HIS BRIDE Maggie Kingsley
THE WOMAN HE'S BEEN WAITING FOR
Jennifer Taylor
THE VILLAGE DOCTOR'S MARRIAGE Abigail Gordon
IN HER BOSS'S SPECIAL CARE Melanie Milburne
THE SURGEON'S COURAGEOUS BRIDE Lucy Clark

August

A WIFE AND CHILD TO CHERISH Caroline Anderson
THE SURGEON'S FAMILY MIRACLE Marion Lennox
A FAMILY TO COME HOME TO Josie Metcalfe
THE LONDON CONSULTANT'S RESCUE Joanna Neil
THE DOCTOR'S BABY SURPRISE Gill Sanderson
THE SPANISH DOCTOR'S CONVENIENT BRIDE
Meredith Webber

MILLS & BOON®

0507 LP 2P P1 Medical

MEDICAL ROMANCE™

Large Print

September

A FATHER BEYOND COMPARE	Alison Roberts
AN UNEXPECTED PROPOSAL	Amy Andrews
SHEIKH SURGEON, SURPRISE BRIDE	Josie Metcalfe
THE SURGEON'S CHOSEN WIFE	Fiona Lowe
A DOCTOR WORTH WAITING FOR	Margaret McDonagh
HER L.A. KNIGHT	Lynne Marshall

October

HIS VERY OWN WIFE AND CHILD	Caroline Anderson
THE CONSULTANT'S NEW-FOUND FAMILY	Kate Hardy
CITY DOCTOR, COUNTRY BRIDE	Abigail Gordon
THE EMERGENCY DOCTOR'S DAUGHTER	Lucy Clark
A CHILD TO CARE FOR	Dianne Drake
HIS PREGNANT NURSE	Laura Iding

November

A BRIDE FOR GLENMORE	Sarah Morgan
A MARRIAGE MEANT TO BE	Josie Metcalfe
DR CONSTANTINE'S BRIDE	Jennifer Taylor
HIS RUNAWAY NURSE	Meredith Webber
THE RESCUE DOCTOR'S BABY MIRACLE	Dianne Drake
EMERGENCY AT RIVERSIDE HOSPITAL	Joanna Neil

MILLS & BOON®

0507 LP 2P P2 Medical